This is a work of fiction. Names, characters, businesses, organizations, places, events and incidents either are the product of the author's imagination or are used fictitiously. Any resemblance to actual persons, living or dead, events, or locales is entirely coincidental.

THE CAPTAIN'S HOUSE

Mel J Wallis

For Mum
As promised, the story of 'The Captain's House'.

CONTENTS

ACKNOWLEDGEMENTS

Who knew a trip to the beach with my girls, Amy and Louise, would result in my first novel, 'The Captain's House'? A quick glance out of the window while stationary in traffic. The neglected house looking so forlorn and unloved. The story was just there.

From that point onwards, the Captain was part of my life and the story just sat in my head ready to be written down.

On some days my family has taken second place to the Captain, when the urge to write has meant dinner was late or not there at all. My husband, Andy, has had to deal with my impatience when the laptop had a mind of its own and did crazy things. He has kept me sane and the writing flowing. Quite honestly, without my family's support, this book would have been started but not finished. Their support has been phenomenal.

I need to mention my wonderful friends, who have read the book in instalments as well as proofread, edited, and offered their ideas as I went along. Particularly Helen, who read my final draft just before leaving the office and missed her train home from work when she got caught up in the story. Karen, who got so involved in the story she invited me for lunch one day just to find out what happened in the next chapter. She needed to know there and then what happened to Mowzer. Anne, who has spent days accompanying me to museums, antique shops, and second-hand bookshops, whose unwavering support and constant encouragement enabled me to have the courage to finish and finally publish the book.

I inherited my love of books and reading from my parents. This book is dedicated to my mum, with whom I first shared the idea of

'The Captain's House' and the ongoing story lines that are continued in the trilogy. Sadly, is she no longer with us to see my idea come into fruition as a 'real' book. She is missed daily and never more so when writing and thinking about the Captain. Or, as I now think of him, my Captain!

One

The house did not look welcoming.

It looked lonely and forlorn. The garden was as unkempt as the house. Rose stood under the large sprawling apple tree and surveyed the garden and house with a critical eye, her hands on her hips. The house was supposed to be empty, but she was sure that she had seen someone moving about inside. There was a slight yellowish glow coming from the back of the house. She was still not sure if she would keep the house or not, and had felt an overwhelming need to come see her inheritance in person, rather than rely on photographs and the boring specifications on the official paperwork that she had been sent. The photographs were appalling too. Grainy, blurry, and out of focus. She wanted the detail, wanted to see behind the dishevelled exterior.

Rose had collected the key from her solicitor that morning and travelled along the main roads to the Kent coast in the rain. She fiddled with the key nervously then decided to brave the wind and rain and leave the shelter of the apple tree behind. Once inside the porch, shielded once more from the rain, Rose inserted the key into the well-worn lock on the left of the solid oak door. The key slotted into the lock and the door swung open to reveal a musty entrance hall with an old armchair propped against the bannisters of the stairs. Rose stepped into the hall and bumped into the brass coat stand, the contents of which wobbled alarmingly, and a sailor's hat fell to the floor.

As she picked up the hat, a single ray of sunshine came through the hallway window, casting a rainbow of colours on the oak floor. The atmosphere changed instantly and the dull oppressive mood within the house lifted. Replacing the hat on the coat stand, she looked at the window and noticed the stained-glass panel at the top of it. A boat was depicted in the panel, and it was this that had produced the rainbow on the floor a moment earlier. It was sailing on a clear blue sea and the sun was shining brightly. Out in the garden there was a small glimmer of sunshine peeking out from the dark grey clouds, mirroring her mood and her growing feelings for the house.

She turned back to the gloom of the hallway and peered into the darkness and the shadows to check that there was no one there, but her. She moved hesitantly around the armchair which had a sunken cushion. It looked as if it had just been vacated. She made her way into the living room. This room was lined with bookcases and had a beautiful, curved window built into the wall, which overlooked a stream running through the garden. The stream was rapidly turning into a fast-flowing river due to the rain. From her vantage point in the doorway, it looked as if the window belonged to a ship and the water, the sea on which it floated. This was definitely a seaman's house, she thought as she looked around her. The house feels and acts like a boat!

Padding back into the hall and onwards into the kitchen, she stared around in dismay. The kitchen was ridiculously small and antiquated, although the built-in cupboards had clearly been designed for and fitted into the tiny space perfectly. There was not much space to swing a cat, but the window was large and would give a stunning view across the garden, once the vegetation had been cleared.

Rose then ventured back into the hallway and climbed the stairs.

She was eager to see what would await her upstairs and thought the views from the second floor would be stunning. She wondered if she would be able to catch a glimpse of the sea. The stairs were bare wood and creaked ominously as her feet landed on every tread.

At the top of the stairs, she was confronted with another stained-glass window, depicting the same boat, this time on the open sea. The waves were rough and high, and the boat was being tossed around. A lighthouse appeared in the corner of the window, offering hope and sanctuary. As she peered through the glass, the brambles and shrubs in the garden knitted together to resemble a stormy sea, matching the image already adorned in the glass.

The landing had three wooden doors leading off it. She pushed open the first door and found it to be a rather untidy bathroom with a peculiar aroma and the prevailing smell of damp. Rose retreated and instead opened the door leading to the back bedroom, which she had hoped would offer views of the countryside and coastline. She was not disappointed. The room was large and spacious. There was a telescope and an old worn leather notebook on the floor in the middle of the room. The notebook looked as though it had been dropped, carelessly discarded just a moment ago. She picked it up and dropped it into her bag to look at later. The sun peeked through the clouds once again, the disturbed dust caught the sunlight and swirled around her in the centre of the room.

Rose was compelled to make her way to the window. Her eyes looked across the river to the land beyond. She caught sight of a man walking along the footpath to the rear of the house. He looked across at the house and spotted her in the window. To her surprise he stopped, waved a hand in greeting, and then continued walking. How odd.

Then, the man stopped, turned back, and waved at her again. He seemed to look directly at her as if he knew her. His eyes met hers and she felt that she knew him, but she could not quite place him. She rested her hands on the glass. Her fingertips seemed to seek their way through the glass and race across the distance to find him. She was drawn to the man in a peculiar way, a physical way even. She looked away to gather her thoughts and when she looked back, he was gone. He had completely vanished, making her question if he was there at all.

She stayed at the window, trying to make sense of what she had just seen, puzzling over where he could have gone. He just seemed to disappear. She took her hands from the glass and saw that she had left an outline of her palms in the grime of the window. It was then that she noticed that she could barely see out. It was raining hard, making it difficult and virtually impossible to see through the glass that was encrusted with dirt, dust, and grime.

Two

The only other room that needed to be explored upstairs was the room at the front of the house. This room was filled with a huge brass bed and a rather lumpy mattress, covered with a charming old-fashioned bedspread with a red rose pattern. There was another armchair in the corner, with a captain's coat hanging off the wing of the chair. Rose sat down in the chair and looked out once again into the garden. The wild space was calling out to be tamed and in her mind's eye she could see how beautiful it could be. She let herself sit there for a while and daydream. She closed her eyes and drifted into a garden with roses and filled with their sweet scent. Then, she felt the ground move beneath her chair. She was rocked gently from side to side, as if the house were a galleon, swaying amongst the waves. Now her nostrils were full of the salty smell of the ocean. Her face was wet with the spray from the waves. When she opened her eyes again, she was not sure if she was on land or sea, but she knew she was home. She had to keep this house. The intensity of her daydreams did not bother her in the slightest, even though she rarely gave herself the time to daydream. Her intense feelings for the house that she had only been inside for less than half an hour did not seem irrational to her at all. She just felt a lazy intimacy with the building and needed to discuss this with somebody, so she returned down the stairs into the hallway.

The wind and rain ceased, and a peaceful calm settled upon the house. Rose stepped into the rickety front porch and telephoned her boyfriend, Mike. He answered after the first ring and it was obvious that he was waiting for her call.

"So how much do you think the house and grounds are worth?" he demanded.

Rose could picture him lounging on his expensive sofa, raising one eyebrow to emphasis his point. It made her blood boil.

She retorted, "I am not sure I will sell, the house is enchanting, and it could look just perfect with a little bit of care and attention."

"Just think of the ready money that would be available right now if you sold it straight on. There is nothing to bind you to the property, it was just your batty aunt that it belonged to. Just get a house clearance firm in and market it as a 'doer upper' or 'with potential'. I have some friends that could market it for you. You don't want to leave it in the hands of some country bumpkin estate agent or solicitor."

His voice had changed and had a whiny nasal twang to it, that showed her exactly what he was thinking.

"I think I will be the judge of that, as it is my property," Rose found herself replying and to her surprise she disconnected the call with a swift swipe of her finger and marched back into the garden. Now the house was making her act out of character. Mike was against Rose keeping the house and wanted her to invest the money in his flagging business. The fact that he had not asked Rose to marry him, or make any long-term commitment, showed his true colours, but now she was determined to follow her dreams. The house was having a strange effect on her. It was making her think hard about her future and questioning her ambitions.

Rose never thought she would have been named in the will of her Great Aunt Lily Anne. The elusive, batty woman who kept herself to herself. Her mum kept a framed photograph of her aunt on the wall in the hallway. It was a pretty photograph of Rose as a babe in arms, cradled lovingly by her Great Aunt Lily Anne in the grounds of this house. She did not remember the last time any of the family had seen or heard from her Great Aunt Lily Anne. She had been told that she was a bewitching character who had suggested the name 'Rose' to her mother who could not decide on a suitable name for her baby. The will had shown her Great Aunt's full name as 'Lily Anne Rose' so now she had a tangible connection with her Great Aunt. Her name.

After the heated conversation with Mike, Rose was adamant that somehow, without any rational explanation, she belonged with the house. She owned the house outright; it was hers and hers alone. She loved living in the hustle and bustle of London in her rented flat, but she also wanted to live right here in this house. The house that was making her dream.

Rose made her way back into the garden to stand under the apple tree once again. She stumbled, and her foot hit something hard in the undergrowth. She reached down and tore the long grass away from the object and was amazed to discover a long wooden bench that had been hidden. With a bit of effort, the bench was once more standing upright. Inscribed in the back of the bench were the words, 'I venture across the seas, but always return to you'. An interesting sentiment and a pertinent statement.

Later, she made another call, this time to her parents and managed to wangle Sunday lunch with them the following weekend. She needed to work out if the house was habitable or would have to be pulled down and rebuilt, and this was a definite 'dad conversation'.

The house was seeping into her very being without her even realising it. She had a vague feeling that the house was owned by a gentleman connected to the sea. She could feel a connection with an old seaman whenever she thought about the house. There was no rhyme or reason for this. No rational explanation. The house was left to her by an old aunt! There was no mention of a man of any age, just an old seaman's hat that she had found, but this man, this connection, was becoming real to her. She knew of no seafaring ancestors.

The following weekend, as she stepped into the neat semi-detached house which was her childhood home, she struggled to understand her feelings for the house. This house was modern and filled with carpets, heating, and large leather furniture, which would not have fitted through the front door of her new house, which was more 'cottage size'. She had never lived in the countryside and her mum and dad's neighbours were just the other side of the wooden fence, not miles away down a lane in the nearest village.

"This is the craziest idea you have ever had," remarked her mum as she greeted her from the kitchen. "Head in the clouds again, whatever are you thinking?"

Her dad walked into the kitchen at this point, wiped his muddy feet on the doormat, and remarked, "Leave her be, Joan. She needs to make her own decisions and she has been left the property. I reckon you should do the property up and see how you feel then."

The banter continued between her parents throughout lunch and the rest of the afternoon. Rose's inheritance – her house – was an interesting conundrum that seemed to pitch people against each other. Her dad was keen for her to keep it, but her mum was wary of the work it would need to make it habitable. Rose's mum was also worried about her daughter, as she could see the effect that the whole debacle was having on Rose already. Rose, however, had changed her outlook on the future and was prepared to start something new, without organizing it to within an inch of its life, as she usually did.

Not much was known of her mum's side of the family tree and no one had really known Great Aunt Lily Anne. Sporadic visits from time to time was all her mum had to tell, together with the photograph of Rose as a baby.

"I haven't the foggiest idea about a gentleman or seaman that lived with your Great Aunt," she puzzled. "I can't think of how or why you have come to that conclusion; a dusty old hat has fired your imagination, my girl, that's all. Perhaps she had a seaman lodger, or she had a seaman to call. She had a reputation of being very feisty in her youth."

When Rose was travelling to work on the train the following day, she realised that she had to take some time away from the office during the next few months as she would need to get the house straight. She vowed to talk to her boss during the morning and talk about taking some leave.

Her mobile phone trilled, and she rummaged in her large roomy handbag to take the call. Taking too much time, she missed the call and, within seconds, her phone trilled once again to let her know she had a text message from her solicitor. 'Looking through the paperwork again for the house and there appears to be a cash settlement as well. Please contact me to discuss. Lee.' The train ground to a halt at the busy London station and Rose found herself pushed towards the ticket barrier in the rush hour crush. A half an hour tube ride later at the office, Rose took a deep breath and called

Lee back.

"Amazing news, Rose," he announced, "we have found an old account of your Great Aunt's, it contains nearly £250,000."

He continued to explain that the terms of the will dictated that, as she was the named beneficiary, she would be entitled to every penny. Rose realised that she could ask for an extended period of leave and it could even be unpaid now, as she had some ready money to play with. The house was good for her, she mused, it was certainly bringing her luck.

Three

In the office, she sat back in her chair and gazed out of the window at the busy London traffic. She caught a glimpse of her reflection in the glass and saw her pensive smile. Swivelling back to face her colleagues scowling at the computer screens and grumbling into the telephone, she knew she was doing the right thing. Grabbing her notebook and reaching for a pen, she drafted a list of all the things she had to include when meeting her boss later in the morning. Time went very slowly as Rose waited, but eventually her computer flashed a timed warning message that her meeting was due to take place in five minutes. 'At last,' she thought, 'it is now or never.' Jumping out of her seat she paced towards her boss's office, she was a woman on a mission!

She was outmanoeuvred by her boss's demeanour as he laughed when she entered his office. "You look like you have won the lottery!" he said. "Or has your long-suffering boyfriend popped the question? Oh no, you are not pregnant, are you?"

She returned his grin and giggled. "No, to all of those, but I do have some good news." Greg, her boss, was a middle-aged portly man who had a secret soft spot for Rose.

His brown eyes sparkled with good humour as he continued to tease her. "Will it be good news for me and the business though?"

Rose outlined her recent good fortune and found herself discussing the house with Greg. Every little detail of the house that she could remember she relayed to him and then, with an impatient sigh, exclaimed, "But should I keep it and can I keep it?"

It was then Greg's turn to laugh; with a bemused grin he exclaimed, "Well, if you don't want it I will have it, perhaps I will even buy it off you, if you want to sell it. The house sounds charming."

She turned to her notebook and read out her list in an official voice. As she came to the end of her 'to do' list, she once more looked out of the window at the bright blue sky and found herself saying, "Would you be able to offer me a lengthy period of unpaid leave?"

"I think you have talked me into it," replied Greg, "but you would need to train up a replacement before you go. Would you mind being available, in case of any dire office emergencies perhaps, on your mobile?"

Rose spent the rest of the day racing around the office, tidying up her files, paperwork, and sorting out one of the younger members of the team, Sarah, to act as her replacement while she was on leave. Rose was confident that after a few days Sarah would be more than able to manage most of her work. She was happy to leave her mobile number just in case. Rose was content that, although her leave was organized, Greg felt that she was important enough to still be contactable while she was away. This made the decision easier.

Later, Rose was getting ready to go out with Lisa, her best friend. She had put this off for a couple of weeks, knowing how crazy her recent decisions would seem to her friend. An old house needing lots of work, taking unpaid leave from the office … Lisa would have taken off around the world blowing the cash on designer clothes and expensive wine. Her friend always told her straight with no frills. Oh yes, many a time while shopping her friend had informed her of her shortcomings in the changing rooms, "No, you can't wear that you look like the back end of the no. 9 bus," or, "Really, do you really need a pudding, where do you put it … oh, I can see where!" Lisa was a rock though, always there through thick and thin, just as a best friend should be. Once her friend had got her head around Rose's decision, she was sure that she would be there for her as she had always been.

Rose had trouble concentrating and time seemed to slip away from her. Her best mate was peering earnestly at her phone as she arrived, slightly late. Lisa jumped up and enveloped Rose in a tremendous hug and announced in a husky whisper, "I am so excited to hear your news, but I'm feeling a bit poorly, so I don't want to stay up all night celebrating!" Glancing around her Rose slipped onto the bench beside Lisa and grabbed the laminated menu, just realising that she had skipped lunch.

"You will have to wait until we have ordered dinner, my stomach feels like my throat has been cut!" Although Lisa pulled a face at having to wait even longer, she let Rose have her way.

When the dinner was ordered, and the drinks were in their hands, Rose excitedly relayed her good news. Rose hurried through the boring estate agent specifications and she gushed over the unique features, the character and dynamics of the property.

"It has a special feel about it. It feels like home and it has a weird and compelling connection to the sea. The stained-glass windows, the telescope in the upstairs bedroom. You can hear the waves crashing onto the shore from the garden. The river flows so close to the house, so the sound of running water can be heard in every room. The wooden panels, furniture, and fitted bookcases make the house feel like the inside of a big ship." She spoke faster and faster, finally pausing for breath and allowing her friend to get a word in edgeways. Lisa was lost for words and took a moment to recap.

"Does that mean that Captain Sparrow will come walking in and whisk you or me away in his arms?" Lisa giggled.

"Well," Rose replied in a whisper, "there was this man that I glimpsed on the footpath opposite the house, when I first went to look at the property. He was drop-dead handsome and he turned to wave at me, as he saw me watching him from the window."

"That speech means that you don't want to run the idea past me for my advice. You are smitten with that house. I have never seen you more excited about anything in your life. Or maybe, your first date with Mike …" Lisa raised her eyebrows at Rose and they both blushed like teenagers.

"Ahem," Lisa pronounced, "a fresh start with a house and your longed for garden. I can't wait to have a look at your house and the view. Will you share it with me?"

Rose retorted, "Listen you, I am willing to share the house with you at weekends, but that handsome man I saw from the window is mine, all mine. If he is single that is. Knowing my luck, he is married with loads of kids and a gorgeous wife!"

Lisa delved into her rucksack and produced a *Country Living* magazine, turning the glossy pages one by one, until she stopped. The pages depicted a cute country cottage, surrounded by flowers and set amid a picturesque valley. The following pages showed kitchens, living rooms, and bathrooms all looking perfect, with all the cushions plumped up and the curtains draped artfully around the window frames.

"Is this your house?"

Rose giggled and grabbed the magazine from Lisa, waving it in the air. "No, no, no. My house is not like that, it is cosy and has *real* character."

Rose spent the entire evening talking about the house with her friend, outlining her plans and visions for the house, but as she travelled home, she knew that she could not change the house too much. For then it would not be the house she had inherited with all its charms. Drifting off to sleep, the last thing on her mind was her mysterious stranger, who had waved at her that day. Her very own house, with its intriguing seafaring past. She pictured the ships depicted on the windows, with their contrasting calm and stormy seas. She was semi awake when the outline of the stranger in her dream morphed into a seaman wearing a sailor's hat. Who was this seaman? What was his connection to the house and her Great Aunt Lily Anne? She was determined to find out.

The house sat in the inky blackness. Silent but not empty. Shadows appeared every now and then in the windows. The shadows were restless and peered out into the distance from behind the glass. Looking for someone or something. The shadows appeared to follow faint glimmers of light. It was candlelight that could be seen which flickered when the breeze caught the flames. What was left of the curtains in the windows also flickered in the light wind which was growing in strength and made the strange light ebb and flow.

The wind continued to grow in intensity and the garden became noisy as the bushes and trees knocked against one another and knitted together to form an impregnable barrier. The house was still, but everything around it was moving wildly. The wind was almost gale force. The shrubs and the gnarled old apple tree bent double by the force. Despite the chaotic night, the shadows were silent at the windows, reassured by the safety of the natural barrier and confident that the wind was unable to penetrate the house.

Someone stood at the entrance to the garden and looked across at the house. They did not attempt to enter the garden as they could feel the force of the wind from where they stood. The man was standing as still as the shadows at the windows and was returning their stares without fear. He was coming back from his daytime wanderings and was hoping to spend the night in one of the outbuildings that belonged to the house. It seemed that he had to wait for everything to die down and the house to welcome him again. The house was waiting for somebody and something, but it was not him. He settled underneath the hedge to wait.

Four

Rose found the next few weeks in the office unbearable. She had trouble focusing on the job, finding herself daydreaming when she should be concentrating. Sarah, her temporary replacement, was very patient with her. Sarah was doing her own kind of daydreaming, but hers was all about promotion and what she would spend all her extra money on. Sarah reminded Rose of what she was like when she started the job. Full of enthusiasm and hot air. Her colleagues in the office were excited for her and her new house, but several of her older colleagues had spoken to her of dry rot, rotten timbers, unsafe stairs and floors. Fred spent the whole afternoon one day describing his nightmare in the year 2000 when his local river flooded and the huge insurance premiums he had paid ever since.

The weather had been dry and sunny since she viewed the house, but now the weather had broken. The weeks that followed were extremely wet and windy, reminding Rose of the day she first visited the house. She wondered how the house was bearing up to the weather and hoped that the wind was not causing any damage. She recalled how flimsy the porch was when she sheltered in it. Rose could not remember the colour of the front door. She wondered whether she would be able to get through the brambles to even find the front door when she returned!

Rose found herself looking for the property's paperwork again. Although she had explored the main building and the garden during her last visit, she was sure that she had missed something. At last she found the paperwork, hidden under a stack of magazines on the coffee table. Amongst the legal paperwork, she found what she was looking for. A map of the property, with the boundaries shown. How had she missed several outbuildings and what looked like a small track leading onto farmland or the surrounding marsh? The bold red line surrounding the house seemed to enclose rather a lot of land and Rose was intrigued by what the buildings might be. Perhaps they were stables, a boat house, or a folly?

It was her last day in the office and her colleagues had begged her for cakes. She stopped at a coffee shop which also sold cakes and pastries and made her way inside. She squeezed between the tables to the main counter. There, she picked a selection of cakes for her friends and colleagues in the office. As she searched in her handbag for her purse to pay for the cakes, she pulled out a photo of the house with it. It fell to the floor of the shop, to be picked up by the lady behind her.

The lady stared at the image of the house and exclaimed, "I know this house. It has been standing empty for years. Are you painting it from this photo, as most artists do?"

Rose turned around to see an older lady, with a friendly round face, framed with a mop of bright ginger hair. She was dressed in a bright raincoat which clashed violently with the colour of her hair. Rose was startled that someone in the middle of London would recognize her house instantly, just from a photograph. She offered to buy the women's coffee and cake in return for her picking up and returning the photo of the house. After paying for their coffee and cakes, she sat down at an adjacent vacant table and carefully tucked the photograph into an inside pocket of her bag. The woman joined Rose at the table. Rose knew she was going to be late for work, but she did not think it would matter too much as it was her last day for a while.

"Hi, I am Rose, and I am the proud new owner of the house in the photo." Rose said as she drew out a chair for the lady to join her.

"Well, that means that I am your new neighbour, as I live a mile or so up the lane from your house. My name is Val."

Val was very interested to learn that the house now belonged to Rose and was thrilled that she was going to renovate and keep it.

"I run 'The Lanterns' as a Bed and Breakfast business with my husband David. 'The Lanterns' is very popular place to stay with artists. Many of our guests have been smitten by your house and spent most of their time with us painting it. Our guests normally wander off to find the beach and stop when they get to your old house," she joked. "They are near some stunning coastal footpaths and beaches, but they spend their time drawn to your house. Did you know that we all refer to your house as 'The Captain's House'? It has been called that by the locals for as long as I can remember," she went on.

Rose remarked that she thought of the house as a seaman's house and told Val that she had found a sailor's hat and jacket when exploring the property. She just knew that they must have belonged to a Captain, but the house was left to her by her Great Aunt Lily Anne.

"Ah ha, old Lily, well that is another story, Rose!" Val laughed. "She was such a character."

Reluctantly, Rose finished her hot drink and looked at her watch. Just as she was finding out what the house was all about, it was time for her leave, as she had to get to the office.

All was not lost as Val pressed her business card into her hand. "You would be very welcome to stay with us anytime, just call me when you are ready to visit the house again. I can fill you in then."

"Well, that would be marvellous," Rose said. "I was planning to go back to the house this weekend and take my mum to see it. We were looking for somewhere to stay."

Val retorted, "I know we have some room then as we had a cancellation just before I left for London. I will ring David, to book you and your mum in."

When Rose entered the office with the requisite cakes, she found Sarah sat at her desk amid a pile of paperwork and filing. Waving her hand at Rose, Sarah continued with her conversation and smiled, motioning her to sit down on another chair with her spare hand. With a sigh, Rose made her way to the tea and coffee machine and placed her cakes on the counter. From nowhere, she was surrounded by a busy throng of people, all talking at once and taking cakes. Greg, her boss, appeared silently at the doorway and a hush fell at once.

"I do believe you are late on your last day," he laughed. "But as you come bearing cakes …" Rose covered her face with her hands, embarrassed. "Oh, I am only teasing, Rose. I am not expecting you to do much today. Sarah seems to have it all covered. After a cup of tea and one of your cakes, I reckon you should go home and start your big adventure," he said with a smile that reached from ear to ear. He patted her on her arm. "We can all see you can't wait to get off."

Rose had always had trouble disguising her feelings and felt very uneasy that everyone knew what she was thinking. She decided not to let it bother her and to enjoy her last day with her friends from the office. After tea and several cakes, Rose said her goodbyes and wandered out through the lobby. She did not have time to be sad, as the journey home was busy, and the train was crowded and packed with commuters. She was wedged between two rather large men for most of the journey and spent the time daydreaming about her time off and what Val's Bed and Breakfast would be like. She decided to look it up on her computer when she got home.

Five

When she arrived home, she retrieved the card with the details of the B and B from her handbag and entered the details into the search engine of her PC. She was surprised to see a large white house set in a formal garden on her screen. She had visions of a small cottage, along the same lines as her house. 'The Lanterns' had several rooms to let with all the trimmings, but it also had a separate holiday let, 'Little Lanterns' – an annexe at the side of the main house. Rose thought it might be cheaper to rent out the annexe for a while, instead of having just a room in in the Bed and Breakfast. After all, she had no idea how long she would be there. Was her house watertight? Did it have running water?

She did not know if Val was staying in London, or was just visiting for the day, but decided to call her just in case. Her husband David answered the phone and stated that Val had just walked through the door. Amazingly, the annexe was available to rent, as Val had just finished re-decorating the main bedroom. It was self-contained, with a small open plan living, dining, and kitchen space and two bedrooms with an en-suite bathroom. Just what Rose needed for the time being.

"What a stroke of luck, I have found what I needed in London today to finish the annexe refurbishment, so you can have it," Val said. "It is yours as long as you need it."

She went on to say that she would make sure she would have it finished by the weekend and looked forward to seeing her Saturday afternoon and meeting her mum.

As Rose traipsed around her London flat, switching the lights on as the night drew in, she thought long and hard once again about her house, and all its surprises. How the dropped photograph in the coffee shop had led her to meet Val and end up lodging with her, just up the lane. She wondered about the people that had stopped to paint the house on their way to the sea. Were they drawn to the house like she was?

The rest of the week passed in a blur and Rose busied herself with getting her London pad tidied up and in 'ship shape' so she could leave it for a while unattended. She popped next door to her neighbour, Iris, to explain that she would be out of town for a while and to ask her to keep an eye on the place for her. Iris was happy to take her post in and pop in every so often.

Iris said, "I bet you will stay down there if it all works out," just as Rose was at her door on her way out. Rose thought long and hard about this before answering with a shy smile, "Maybe."

It was so easy for Rose to imagine the house all done up and cosy, and she wondered if she would ever have anyone special who would want to share it with her.

Rose was waiting in for her shopping to be delivered, when her mobile trilled and a message popped into her in box. It was from Mike, asking her if he could pop around to see her that evening. It was crazy, she thought, that she would drop everything, including Mike, to traipse to an unknown part of Kent to a strange house without a second glance. Perhaps she needed that second glance, so she texted him back asking him to come around in about an hour.

She put her shopping into the cardboard box that she planned to take with her, so that she could take it to her car in a bit. Mike came through her front door that she had left ajar so she could get through with her shopping. He enveloped her in a big hug and planted a huge smacker of a kiss on her cheek.

"Got here just in time, I am here to persuade you to come to the States with me on business next week. That decrepit old house can wait. I am set to make a mint if I can make good on this deal. You could make that happen with me."

Rose wriggled out of his arms and stood facing him, legs apart and hand on her hips. "Really, seriously?"

She outlined her plans for the next couple of months and stood back and waited for the explosion of emotion. Mike was a very emotional man and he was certainly not going to leave it there.

He stared at her in disbelief and shook his head. "I reckon you could be persuaded, and you have already got the time off work. Fantastic."

He smiled. It was only then that Rose looked down and noticed the pizza box and bottle of wine in his hands. Mike looked around for somewhere to put the wine and pizza and he suddenly noticed that the small living space was covered in boxes. Every spare space had something on it already. He picked up her groceries and almost dropped them on the floor with his impatience. He placed the bottle of wine and the pizza on the table. "I am going to need a bottle opener and two glasses then you and I are going to toast my success. That old house can wait," he stated firmly with a wry smile. Her amorous boyfriend took her in his arms and looked down at her with a big smile. He glanced across to the bedroom and let her go, grabbing her arm and then pulling her gently to the door. Mike was doing his level best to persuade Rose to go with him and was pursuing every angle. She wriggled free from him for a second time, with a sigh.

It then took Rose the best part of two hours to convince Mike that she was leaving for Kent the following day and was not going to change her plans just for him.

"I have been stating the obvious all evening," she cried for the millionth time. "I am going to stay in a bed and breakfast near my new house and spend some time working out what the house needs to make it livable again and how much it is all going to cost. Who knows, perhaps I will even move down there if everything goes well? I love the old, decrepit house and I feel a weird connection with it. I am having trouble feeling any connection with you, right now," she exclaimed. "You are not listening to me at all. Have you ever listened to me? It is all about you, isn't it?"

Mike paced the floor and picked up the now empty pizza box off the floor on his way out and slung it in the direction of her kitchen bin in temper, as he left. He issued an ultimatum, "You will have to make a choice, the house or me. I am not planning on staying or living in the wilds of Kent anytime soon, even for a dirty weekend!"

Six

Rose climbed into bed, looking around at the tidy space. Her bedroom had never been this tidy, even when she was a little girl. She was always too busy finding the perfect outfit in double quick time, tossing the rejected garments around her. Her bed and floor were always covered in an array of items, from underwear to jackets, smart shoes to flip flops. Mike always joked that she was always surrounded by a 'sea of mess'. How ironic, she mused at another nautical expression. She was subconsciously thinking of the house again. She rolled onto her side and wished she could have smoothed things over with Mike. The bed was large and cold, and she wanted someone to cuddle and make a fuss of her. Mike would have been only too happy to stay the night. He was so eager to persuade her to follow his plans. Rose wished she had let him. But she knew that she would have got no reassurance from him that she was doing the right thing. Mike had tried to tempt her with his plans for his international business in the States all night. Fancy hotels, smart clothes, fast cars, and a life of luxury was what he had planned. Not a little cottage in rural Kent. Rose was not even sure that he wanted a partner and a home to return to, just a woman on his arm, when and where he needed or wanted her.

She thought of the bench that she found in the garden with its poignant words carved carefully into the back. 'I venture across the seas, but always return to you'. Would that be Mike, when he had got his crazy business ideas out of his system? Was he the man for her? Or would she meet the handsome man that she spied from the house on her last visit again in the future? He seemed to know her, and she had certainly not forgotten him. Where did he go? He seemed to vanish into thin air.

The next day Rose woke up, jumped out of bed, and peered excitedly out of the window. She was eager to see what the weather was like and if it was dry. She did not fancy a long car journey in the rain. The wet weather always seemed to dampen her spirits, although it was a horrible, wet, and windy day when she saw the house for the first time. She could see that the weather was dry, with the promise of some sunshine. It could not be better for the journey and Rose wanted to show the house off to her mum. She desperately wanted her mum's approval. She knew that once her mum had decided she liked it, she would be on her side through thick and thin. Rose was sure that she faced many obstacles before she could call the house her home. She desperately wanted to have her mum on her side.

Her dad was the more pragmatic of her parents and was treating the house as a way of making money. His idea of doing the property up and making the garden look nice, just to buy another bigger property, was prompted by all the television programmes that he pretended not to watch in the evenings. Her dad had lots of friends in the building trade and promised to help her out with any DIY stuff that he could deal with. He was not the world's best at DIY, but he knew plenty of people that were. His friends had helped him out of several DIY disasters and Rose could not help but recall the time her dad put his foot through the ceiling and brought a shower of plaster over their heads while they were watching the TV one evening.

After a quick shower, she dressed and started to pack the car with the groceries she had sorted out the evening before. She came across the discarded pizza box on the floor next to the bin and with a sigh put it with the empty wine bottle in a black sack outside. She decided to text Mike when she arrived and let him have her new address. Should she give him the address of her new house or the address of 'The Lanterns' annexe? Should she call her new house 'The Captain's House', as it seemed to be known as in the village, or did the house have another name hidden in the undergrowth? Perhaps there was a board with the name of the house somewhere on the broken fence around the property obscured by the ivy and hedging?

As she locked the front door and put the keys in her jeans pocket, she turned to wave at Iris, who was putting her empty milk bottles on her step. Her stomach was churning the way it does on Christmas morning, full of excitement. Or it could be that she was hungry, as she had packed the breakfast things in the box and not eaten. She grabbed a packet of chocolate Hobnobs from the box on the back seat of the car and munched a couple on the way to pick up her mum.

Her mum was waiting at the window as she pulled up in the driveway. She had her coat on and was opening her front door before Rose could turn the engine off. Laughing at her mum's keenness to get going, she met her on the drive and greeted her with a kiss on the cheek. Her dad had heard her drive up and followed her mum out of the doorway with two large bags in his hands.

"I think your mum is leaving me. She is taking enough for a month or two. Send her back when you have had enough," he said, joining in the laughter before adding, "I will pop over during the week, to have a look for myself."

"I knew he could not resist a peek before long," her mum replied.

Seven

As Rose followed the weekend traffic towards the Kent coast, she felt like she didn't have a care in the world. She had her mum with her, singing badly to the radio, and she did not have to think about work for the foreseeable future. She had a healthy bank balance and an adventure ahead of her. Realistically, she thought, she could end up returning to London with her tail between her legs and a miserable bank balance. Her financial good fortune could be gobbled up by the house and all the work that it needed. Rose stopped worrying when her mum finished the chorus to 'Wake Me Up Before You Go-Go' with a mournful wail. She was still hungry and pulled up at a roadside cafe for a bacon sandwich. Her mum demolished a full English breakfast, as she munched on her sandwich. The cafe had a small shop selling local Kentish produce, guidebooks, and maps. Rose bought a OS map of the area and a local guidebook. Her mum picked up a local newspaper and announced that they would find out any of the local goings on and plenty of gossip from that.

A short while later, after travelling through a maze of lanes with high hedges, they were parked alongside a country pub, puzzling over the map. Rose found she had to turn the map the direction they were travelling, so she could find her way. "It would help if we could find out where we are," announced her mum. "Perhaps you should have borrowed your dad's sat-nav thing?"

Rose replied, "I found the house just fine the first time I visited. It might be your singing that has put me off."

They agreed to turn the radio off and attempted to follow the map. After having to turn around numerous times in farmyards, passing places, and having to do a 10-point turn in the narrowest lane you could imagine, Rose eventually edged the car into the driveway of Val and David's house. A large white house surrounded by a formal garden with woodland to the rear in the distance.

"I thought we were going to your house first, Rose," her mum sighed as she clambered inelegantly out of the car. Rose paused to catch her breath and her temper, retorting in double quick time that "All good things come to those that wait!"

A tall, bespectacled man came out to greet them.

"You must be Rose, and this must be your mum, Joan. Welcome to 'The Lanterns'. I am David, Val's better half!"

David was very tall, and Rose felt quite intimidated standing next to him. David smiled and shook her hand enthusiastically, until Rose felt that if he pumped her hand any more she would have water coming out of her ears. Val came racing down the steps to greet Rose and her mum, almost tripping over in the haste to beat David to his greeting.

"Out of the way, David," she cried, "they are my new guests – get your own."

As they walked across the drive to the side annexe, Val and David bickered about who brought in the most guests and which of them had the most engaging personality. Rose and her mum exchanged sideways glances at each other and wondered what they had let themselves into. Val threw open the door of the annexe and stood back to gauge their reactions. Val had put a lot of effort into the design of the annexe and was hoping for good reactions from her new guests.

She was not disappointed as Joan gasped, "This is like something in a magazine. Oh, how wonderful. You need to make friends with this woman and borrow some of her design flair for your little house."

Rose agreed with her mum, "My ideas for the house are a little different, I want to retain all the character and essence of the property just as it is. I need to preserve the nautical touches."

David looked pensive. "Are you referring to the old Captain himself? Your house is named after a captain. It has been said that your house was a home to generations of seamen and captains. You sound like you want to pickle a captain and put him on display on your mantelpiece!"

"I would settle for a painting, old photograph, or something similar of the Captain over the fireplace," retorted Rose.

Val laughed, "Most of our guests have painted or taken photographs of that old place, that should not be a problem! Not sure what the Captain looks like, but there are plenty of locals that have claimed they have seen him at the window."

Joan injected that she had not seen the old place yet and was dying for a glimpse of the house, let alone the ghostly Captain himself.

David unpacked the car for them and put their box of groceries on the table. Handing Rose the keys to the door and the gate at the end of the driveway, he left them to it. Val had already left and was making up a cream tea for them in her big kitchen. Without the chatter of David and Val, the large living space suddenly seemed very quiet. Rose and her mum faced each other across the laden table, looking over the top of the cardboard box piled high with groceries. Rose felt silly to have packed food in the first place, as there was bound to be a supermarket that sold the same stuff, at least half an hour away.

It all seemed so real to Rose at that very moment; a new albeit temporary place to live and her new Captain's House to keep her busy and give her something to spend her money on. It was time to get to know her new life and stop just dreaming it. The silence was broken by Val entering the room with a large tray laden with scones, jam, and an indecent pot of clotted cream and a pretty, floral teapot with a tea cosy in the shape of a Kent Oast House.

"You need something to eat before you go to poke around that old house. You will find the time disappears with you and you will come back much later than you imagined."

"Would you like to join us this afternoon, Val?"

Val declined with a smile. "I'll pop around another day to see how you are getting on. You call me if you need anything at all though."

After stuffing themselves for the second time that day and discussing how much weight they would put on if they continued to eat this way, they locked the front door of the annexe and set off down the lane to the Captain's House.

Eight

It was warm and bright in the early spring sunshine. Rose and Joan walked up the lane to the house expecting to enjoy views of the countryside and maybe a glimpse of the sea, but they could not see anything over the high hedges that were lining the fields. When they came across an old wooden gate, they both leaned on the top of it and drank in the view. The land was very flat and the hedge was the last structure to obscure the view. The grazing sheep became specks of white as Rose and Joan looked over the gate into the far distance and were rewarded by a tantalising glimpse of the sea.

Rose felt nervous and could feel hundreds of butterflies dancing around in her stomach. "I hope you like the house, mum," she mumbled. Joan took her daughter's hand and dragged her along, like a reluctant toddler to play group.

"I am sure I will like the house, it's just everything that goes with it that worries me. Not to mention your ghostly Captain."

All at once, they were right there, at the boundary of the Captain's House.

"Oh, it is as pretty as a picture. I can see why you fell in love with it," her mum exclaimed with a gasp.

"It's so 'chocolate boxy', but I can see there are some chocolates missing," she pointed to the chimney stack that was leaning to the left, "and some missing roof tiles!"

They giggled at the chocolate analogy together as they went through the gate. Standing once more under the apple tree, but this time not alone, Rose looked again at the house that was now officially hers. She had the keys in her hand and, glancing up at the bedroom window, all you could see through the cloudy dirty glass was a sailor's coat hanging precariously on the wing of the old armchair.

Her mum followed her gaze and shivered. "I can see why they call it the Captain's House, is it really haunted, do you think?"

"My Captain is a friendly fellow I hope, mum," said Rose, picking her way through the long grass and weeds to the house and unlocking the door.

Pushing the door inwards, and stepping into the house once again, Rose sighed and looked around. Nothing much had changed, but it needed some fresh air, so they left the front door open as they both explored the downstairs. Rose heard Joan let out a loud groan as she peered into the tiny kitchen. The beautiful curved wooden window seat overlooking the river was so inviting, Rose had sat down and did not join her mum in the kitchen to lament the lack of space. Once again, she was swept away by the view from this window. The garden was so wild that the vegetation was almost as high as the window and a sapling knocked against the glass, as if it was trying to get her attention. The carpenter who had worked on this room had created wooden panels and bookcases, together with the window seat, and it all flowed together to resemble a cabin in a ship, perhaps at the back of a galleon. Rose knew nothing of a nautical or maritime nature, but she was keen to find out. She reasoned that the house could have been based on or around a ship, as which sailor wants to spend time on land? She wondered where all the books were that would have lined the shelves. If they had been here, they could have offered her an insight into the house's past.

A loud thump startled Rose and she rushed to the source of the noise, colliding with her mum on the way. The front door had slammed shut and in doing so had knocked a hat from the stand in the hallway to the floor. She picked up a peaked Captain's hat and replaced in on the stand, slightly spooked, as the very same hat fell off the brass coat stand the last time she was here. The Captain seemed to be very much in situ.

They both retreated up the stairs and her mum considered the bathroom with another wry look of her face. She wrinkled her nose in disgust as the overwhelming smell of damp and something unidentifiable assailed her nostrils. Rose gently led her mum into the large back bedroom, which was largely empty, with a telescope pointing at the window. This room was above the living room and when they looked down at the waist-high weeds they looked just like the sea, ebbing and flowing around a ship.

Rose could not help but look for the man that she saw the last time she was in this room. Across the river there was an elderly gentleman walking an equally elderly brown and white spaniel with a slow measured pace along the track beside the river. He did not see Rose in the window, so there was no need to wave. Rose was dismayed but not surprised that the handsome man was not walking at that very same moment along the track once again. She felt a fool for even thinking of him at all, together with his cheeky knowing wave. As she looked out of the window, she remembered how she felt when she glimpsed the waving stranger. How her heart pounded and her skin tingled. If she stared hard enough, she could see him again. Her mind was playing tricks on her. He was there, once more looking at her, meeting her gaze, as if they knew each other. Her body felt decidedly odd and she paced once again to the window without realising it, hands once again on the actual pane, palms down. The cold glass shook her from her dreaming and made her brain focus on what she was looking at. The man with his elderly dog swam into her view with a shake of her head. Rose was pleased that her mum had left the room and she did not have to explain her behaviour. Rose took a closer look at the telescope. She was very tempted to look through the lens of the telescope, but she was frightened at what she would see. Would she see reality or something or someone else? However, she could not resist for long and knelt in the dust and dirt and attempted to peer through the lens. All she could see was the grey, thick dust on the lens that was obscuring her view. She tried to move it, to examine the telescope in more detail, but it appeared to be stuck fast and propped into position, looking at a spot in the distance. The telescope appealed to her nosy nature and she was sure that she would be able to see the boats in the distance once she knew how to work it and had cleaned it up.

Nine

The front bedroom with the big bed with its brass adornments and floral bedspread captivated her mum.

"Oh, what a lovely room, and that bedspread is so cute. The large roses are so feminine. Here is the female influence, this room is a dream. I can't believe that this was your batty Great Aunt Lily Anne. You must keep this bed, but that lumpy mattress will have to go. We will have to check inside and underneath before we throw it away, there could be something hidden in there. You never know."

Rose believed that the house was beginning to catch her mum in its spell. She remembered that she had spent some time in this room, sitting in the old armchair, and it was here that she made her decision to keep the house. It seemed to invoke so many emotions for such a small property. As they made their way back down the stairs, stopping to admire the stained-glass windows on the way, there was a knock at the front door.

Rose opened the front door to reveal a short, stocky man with a disheveled appearance. He was wearing an old, beige coat tied in the middle with a piece of parcel twine. Underneath the coat she could see an equally dirty pair of grey trainers. He waved his fist at Rose and yelled at the top of his voice, "You should go back to where you came from and leave the house right now! This house needs to be left alone," he implored her, his voice becoming whinier and wheezier by the minute.

Rose was horrified, but interested to find out why, but before she could gather her thoughts together, her mum had pushed her out of the doorway and was coaxing the man down the path towards the gate that was hanging from the gatepost by a whisker.

"I am sure you mean well, but this house belongs to Rose. You have no right to frighten her, if you won't go, I will call the Police."

As Rose raced to catch up with her mum and the man, she knew that she had made the right decision not to tell her mum about her experiences in the back room overlooking the river. Her mum was in protective mode and she did not want to worry her.

Rose caught up with them both at the gate. "What's your name?" Rose asked the man.

The man replied, "My name is Christian. I belong here. I have lived around here all my life. Way longer than you! This house is haunted, and no one wants to live here because of the Captain."

Rose was perplexed as she was convinced that *her* house and its past was all good. She reasoned that the property was left to her and was even more determined to find out more when she could. Christian calmed down when he knew that Rose wanted to talk.

"Some of the local people have claimed to see a Captain in the house and its grounds. The Captain has different appearances, wearing several naval uniforms with different insignias and hats," he said.

Rose asked, "Are his actions or appearances sinister in any way?"

"No one has ever hung around long enough to find out, but I shelter in the building over there in the cold months of the year, so I know so much more than everyone else. The buildings are watertight but stuffed with old nautical junk and other bits and pieces."

Rose was keen to find out more. "What more do you know about the house?" she asked, her speech coming out louder and faster as she grew more excited, but her further questions fell on deaf ears, as Christian was distracted by a car coming along the lane beside them. He hurried away without saying goodbye and seemed to have forgotten them already.

Joan clutched the gate post with one hand and as she did so the gate collapsed in front of her. "Stop wrecking the place, mum," Rose cried. They both manhandled the gate to the side of the driveway with difficulty, but in gales of laughter. Her mum's laughter betrayed the tense, worried look in her eyes as she watched Christian shuffle off into the distance.

"This place is going to need lots of tender loving care, and I do hope that Captain of yours extends some to you. What do you make of that Christian guy? Do you want him living in your outbuildings next winter?" Rose pondered the questions. She deliberately ignored the main question that was hidden in the middle of her mum's questions. It was a trick that used to baffle Rose as a child, but she had got wise to her mum's sneaky ways of getting her to unintentionally answer her questions.

"I think he is harmless, and he seems to have plenty of information about this old place. I must ask Val where I can find him again."

They turned around and looked back at the house, which looked serene in the sunshine. It was hard to imagine anything sinister happening here. Then, her mum noticed the bench that Rose found last time. She sat down gingerly on the bench, expecting it to give way anytime. It held her weight, so she beckoned her daughter to sit by the side of her. Rose sat down and Joan attempted to explain her feelings to her daughter.

"I feel the same way about the house as you. I am, however, extremely worried about how much money it would take to make it habitable and eventually a home."

They looked around at the garden and tried to work out where the boundaries of the property were. The hedges at the front of the property running alongside the road were easy to identify as the border. Everything else was not so easy, as there was no fencing at the back or sides of the property. The garden was only partially enclosed by large shrubs and trees. It was difficult to make out as the garden was really a jumbled mess of vegetation. Rose had forgotten to bring her property documents and the map showing the boundaries in red.

"We should bring the documents and walk the boundary the next time we visit," Rose said.

As Rose looked up at the window for the second time that day, she caught another glimpse of the coat on the back of the chair, or was it the Captain? As she stared the house seemed to pull her in, was it something to be feared? She did not think so, but she could not be sure.

If she had glanced back as they walked away, she would have seen a definite shadow at the window, a hand raised in greeting and then knocking on the glass to get their attention. There was no noise to accompany the knocking, but the glass was shaking. The window was shaking. The vibrations snaking their way across the glass.

Ten

When they got back to 'Little Lanterns' the evening was drawing in. They spent the evening settling into the annexe, unpacking and making themselves comfortable. Rose cooked a light supper that they ate in front of the television. Neither of them was really watching the programme, which was an old film from the eighties. Rose was trying to think practically about the house and all that needed to be done. Her mind kept turning to the Captain and the Captain's hat that insisted on falling to the floor whenever she was in the building. Perhaps it was the shape of the coat from the upstairs window that was convincing all the locals that there was someone up there looking out. Bizarre.

Joan, on the other hand, was dreaming of soft furnishings and curtains to match the lovely, old floral bedspread in the front bedroom. She had put a new oven in the kitchen and squeezed a fridge in the corner but, realising that there was not any room for any washing appliances, she thought of the outbuildings and wondered if they were any electricity in there. Her mind kept coming back to the state of the roof and the missing roof tiles, the pungent smell in the bathroom, and of course the words of warning from the strange, disheveled character, who went by the name of Christian. She resolved to speak to Val about him in the morning.

The following morning, Rose was up first and checked her mobile phone, as was her habit, checking for last minute e-mails/messages from the boss. She felt a little uneasy when she remembered that she no longer had to do so, but still resolved to check it every day in case they needed her advice. She was sure that Sarah would not need to call her and certainly would not call her unless she really had to, as she would probably consider that a personal failure. Sarah was welcome to her job for a while, Rose thought, she was looking forward to the break and spending time with her mum back at the house. She was only down the lane and she thought she could pop along to the house if she wanted to before breakfast. Unfortunately, her mobile started to ring just as she was putting it back down. She wished she had not answered it when she started a long, involved conversation with Mike, who was at the airport and bored. Rose knew he was just filling in time, as he explained that his plane was delayed. He was half heartily trying to persuade Rose to join him, but was quickly aware that he was flogging a dead horse. He asked her about the house and made a note of the 'Little Lantern' address to keep in touch. Rose did not give him the details of the Captain's House, nor did she tell him that the B and B was just down the lane. She did not want him turning up unannounced and turning her dream sour, with a wilting glare and a 'told you so' expression. She overheard his flight being called and he rang off abruptly as she had expected.

Joan had overheard the conversation and greeted her daughter with a hug. Switching the kettle on, she bustled about the kitchen making Rose a much-needed cup of tea and she tipped muesli and cereal into breakfast bowls. They munched companionably and chatted about the weather and other neutral subjects while they ate. Then, Joan questioned Rose about her relationship with Mike. Rose knew this was coming by her mum's expression over breakfast. She outlined Mike's views on the house and her windfall. She went on to explain that he had wanted her to invest in his business and keep him company in the States. Joan, although fond of Mike, was pleased that her daughter was being so sensible and not being taken in by Mike's patter and promises. Mike was textbook good-looking, blond hair, blue eyes and a wide smile, but you could not trust him as far as you could throw him. Joan was sure that a few thousand miles between Rose and Mike for a couple of months would show if the relationship was steady and able to survive. Rose would have her mind taken off Mike with the house and it was likely her daughter's life would be changed considerably by the time Mike was back in the country again.

Rose spread the documents for the house over the table when they had finished breakfast and cleared away. They spent the morning poring over them. It was plain to see in the survey and maps of the house that there was some land that belonged to the property and several outbuildings. There was a track marked on the map that Rose recognised as the footpath that ran alongside the river.

Later that day, Rose and her mum spent an enjoyable afternoon tramping around the garden and the land adjoining the property, working out where everything was. The outbuildings were bigger than expected and Rose felt her excitement growing once again. They did not have time that day to look at everything hidden under the dust sheets in the outbuildings, but Rose was sure that she might find some of the missing contents of the Captain's House hidden away. Maybe she would find his books and his secrets relating to his sea-faring past?

The contents of the outbuildings were wrapped up tight to protect them from the elements. Within the house other items were hidden to keep them safe and to make sure that they would only be discovered at the right time by the right person. They belonged to the past and the present and they were hidden in the dark. Waiting.

Eleven

Rose caught up with Val in the village shop the following day, as she was picking up some more groceries and another local newspaper. Val chastised her, "You should have told me that you would like a newspaper in the morning, I am happy to collect a newspaper for you when I pop out for mine and the other guests. I love to fuss over people," Val exclaimed, "you only have to ask." Rose thanked her and they strolled back to 'Little Lanterns' together. It was an excellent opportunity for her to find out more about the area and discover if Christian was as sinister as his appearance suggested.

To her surprise, Val did not know that much about Christian. He came and went from time to time, did not do any harm, and seemed to cope well with sleeping rough. Val was unaware that he slept in the Captain's House outbuildings during the winter months.

Rose said, "Christian implored me to leave the house alone. Do you think that he would cause any trouble if I don't?"

"I would not have thought so, he seems harmless, don't you think?"

"Yeah, harmless," replied Rose.

They concluded that Christian seemed to want to care for the house as well, so they should get along just fine. Christian wandered around the local area and had his favourite spots around the village and by the sea. It seemed that Rose would have no trouble finding him again if she needed to.

Val voiced her thoughts, she explained that it was more likely that Christian would find Rose, before too long, and he would make his intentions clear.

"I don't think that you should visit the house alone for a while, at least until you have caught up with Christian. If you must, carry your mobile phone and make sure it is charged," she chuckled, as she remembered that her own mobile was never charged.

Val was amazed to discover that Rose and her mum had not been to see the sea since they had been staying at the annexe. Most of her guests just dropped off their bags and rushed off to the beach the moment they arrived. Although, she added, her other guests were not as lucky as Rose to have been given the Captain's House which was surely a big distraction to the sea. As they walked past the Captain's House, on their way back to 'The Lanterns', Val noticed that gate was missing. "You are supposed to be fixing the house?" she teased.

Rose found her mum looking at the local map when she returned, munching on a piece of toast. She recounted her conversation with Val to her mum, over a cup of tea.

"You know the house is walking distance from the sea. I think we should visit the beach today and explore the area. Let's have an adventure."

Rose decided to take the car so that they were not tempted to stop once again at the house. Rose and her mum had not done anything to the house or garden since they had arrived. They had wandered around talking about their plans and trying to imagine what it had looked like when the Captain lived there and identifying plants in the garden. Nothing useful. Rose resolved to make a list of all the repair jobs that needed doing on the house sometime soon, at least before her dad arrived mid-week. The leaning chimney and missing roof tiles would be at the top of her list.

It was a short drive to the beach, across the flat landscape. They arrived at a shingle beach with a large expanse of sand stretching into the distance. Rose parked the car by the side of the road and they set off to explore the beach. There were a few fishing boats pulled up on the bank of shingle and a small hut which contained the winching equipment to take the boats to and from the water. There was a sharp, salty breeze and Joan pulled her jacket tight around her as they crunched down the shingle towards the sea. The closer they got to the sea, the more the wind picked up and their hair whipped in to their faces. Standing staring at the sea, Rose wondered if her Captain had been a fisherman and if he would have kept a boat right here on the shingle bank or if he had been a Merchant Navy man with a big ship that sailed the world. She pondered that he could have been both, maybe he retired and became a fisherman, so he could still sail the seas and catch something for supper …

This part of the beach was not for tourists, as it did not have anything to encourage people to stop and look around. It was the working part of the beach, for the fisherman. Rose spied some other buildings in the distance. Rose and Joan continued to walk alongside the sea to find out what they were. The wooden rectangular buildings housed shops selling cream teas, ice creams, fish and chips and seaside souvenirs. There were also toilets and the usual 'Pay and Display' car park that brought some much-needed revenue for the local Parish Council.

Rose thought that the beach would get very busy in the summer months, English weather permitting. Parking would not be easy, so she would have to see where her footpath went to. She imagined that it would come out somewhere near the fisherman's end of the beach. The map had been forgotten so they would have to leave it to another day, or walk it from the other end, from the Captain's House and see where they would end up. Rose thought this would be a better idea. She liked the idea that she would be walking in the Captain's footsteps.

Rose remembered the telescope that was facing the sea in one of the upper bedrooms, that it was fixed in position. She had not moved it yet, as they had always walked to the cottage from 'Little Lanterns'. Perhaps it was fixed on this part of the ocean. Was it used by the lady of the house to watch for her lover coming home or was the Captain a smuggler watching for his illegal contraband to be brought safely into shore?

Twelve

The days that followed passed in a blur for Rose as she and Joan kept themselves busy compiling a list for her dad of all the things that needed fixing in the house. That was if they focused on the job in hand. Often, they ran off the plot, wondering about rugs, curtains, and the all-important garden. They sat side by side on the bench, taking numerous breaks, chatting about soft furnishings and if the house should be painted white, cream, or something more unusual.

The list for dad grew longer and longer as the house was in urgent need of repairs everywhere and in every room. The roof leaked in the bathroom, which was the reason for the terrible damp smell, but it was suspected that something may have died under the floorboards as well as the smell was so pungent. The chimney was the main concern as it seemed to tilt at a funny angle which looked quite charming from the garden. Rose doubted that her dad would find it charming at all. The floorboards creaked ominously which seemed to suggest that they could be rotten. The bannister up the stairs wobbled if you gripped it too hard. All the taps in the property dripped and, when it rained, all you could hear was drip, drip, drip from every room in the house. However, the views from the house were stunning even when it rained. Rose always looked out over the river to the footpath, hoping for a glimpse of her handsome stranger.

She often found herself gazing into the distance at the sea glinting on the horizon and sometimes fancied that she could hear the crashing of the waves on the shingle beach from the house.

Rose was daydreaming at the window, picturing the garden in its summer splendour in her mind's eye, when she heard a man's voice from below, calling her name. At first, she was startled, but then she recognised the familiar tone. Her dad had finally made it to the house. Her stomach started to squirm inwardly as she rushed down the stairs to greet him. Her mum had got there first and opened the heavy oak door to let him in.

"Wow, what a lovely little place you have here, sweetheart," he called up the stairs to Rose. "Beautiful house, even in this state," he exclaimed. Rose took him by the hand and led him into the main room in the house overlooking the stream and footpath towards the coast. Her dad was taken aback by the workmanship of the bookcases and the window seat and ran his fingers along the wood as he walked around the room.

"I can see why you wanted to keep the house; it has a character all of its own."

Her dad left her and continued to explore the house on his own and returned to the main room, holding the Captain's hat in his hands.

"This fell off the banister as I walked past. Silly place to put it," he said. He placed the hat in the middle of the mantelpiece. "It should stay put there."

Rose explained, "Wherever that hat is put it always falls to the floor when I am in the house. I think it's the Captain making his presence known."

Her dad frowned at Rose and her mum, who had just joined

them. "Are you suggesting that the house is haunted, love?" he questioned.

"The locals seem to think so, especially Christian. I believe the Captain wants me to have the house and does not want to be forgotten," Rose replied.

"Who is Christian?" her dad said. "You have not mentioned him in my daily updates, Joan?" he said, as he turned to face his wife.

She shook her head at him. "He is just a man who sleeps rough in the outbuildings here in the winter. He seems harmless enough and Rose is not bothered by him, Pete."

As her dad left the house and continued to explore the garden, he could be heard muttering to himself that he needed to check this Christian out.

Eager to distract her dad, Rose followed him out to the garden and showed him the bench that she had found on her first visit to the house hidden in the brambles. She invited him to sit down with a sweep of her arm, pointing out the inscription engraved into the back of the bench as they sat down. She handed her dad the list that she had complied with the help of her mum and waited with impatience for his response. He laughed at her entry for the chimney, 'chimney stack needs to be put right, but quite like the funny angle'.

"Yeah, right. That nice, funny angle will cost you nice funny money," he said as he looked at her with a grin.

She fell silent as he continued to read. He explained that he had invited some of his friends down that afternoon and they would give him some idea of the cost and timescales of the work needed on the house.

Reassured that her dad meant well, Rose and her mum decided to leave her dad at the house to meet his friends and go back to the annexe of 'Little Lanterns' to keep out of the way. Rose's dad would drop into the annexe afterwards and let Rose know the extent of the work and the good or bad news.

Rose spent the afternoon pacing the floor of the annexe and wondering what her dad and his builder friends were making of her house. Would she be able to afford to keep it, or would it be so expensive to put right that she would have to sell it on to someone else when the work was done? She vowed that she would do everything she could to keep the house.

Thirteen

Rose spent the next few days worrying about money and contacting the local builders for quotes for all the work that was needed to make the house habitable, as she would have to wait a while for her dad's friends in the building trades to finish their current work. Rose did not want to wait. She was keen to get started.

Rose and her dad had chatted through the long list of work when he had returned after his visit, talking into the small hours. Her dad offered his DIY skills, but admitted that she needed to get some professionals in. He agreed that speed was of the essence, going on to explain that he was not sure that the house was very safe. He was very worried about the wonky chimney and lamented that if it were to topple it would crash through the roof and smash through his favourite room of the house, the living room with the window seat and impressive woodwork.

When her dad left, he gave her a massive hug and whispered in her ear, "Stick with it, love, I will help you out as much as I can."

However, for the very first time since she decided to keep the property, Rose suffered sleepless nights. She found herself walking around the small kitchen of the annexe in the early hours, wondering if she had done the right thing, if the money was going to last and thanking her lucky stars that she had only asked for a career break and not chucked in her job. Her only saving grace was her mum, who was there for her in the morning, tempting her to eat a breakfast and get on with the day. Every day brought more worry and more costs and Rose felt that her dream was being taken over by reality.

During the nighttime hours, the shadows at the house were still, there was no movement and no lights wandering around the house and at the windows. There was a warm glow at the back of the property and the only light that was seen was a red glow that could be glimpsed from time to time, as if someone was smoking a pipe sitting in the upstairs armchair looking across the fields towards the Lanterns.

It was her mum's last day. Rose had a visit to the house lined up to meet a local man called Steve who was recommended by Val and David. Steve owned a local property maintenance firm and was prepared to give a tentative preliminary quote for all of the work as he subcontracted to other local tradesman. He would assist with the renovations and manage the day-to-day building work. Rose hoped and prayed that he was an amenable guy as this seemed like the perfect solution to all her problems.

Being a typical mum, Joan had seen that Rose was stressed and extremely worried about the future of the Captain's House. Joan had decided that she would spend the morning at the annexe packing to go home, but secretly she was planning to make a hotpot meal and tidy the annexe, doing the jobs that Rose hated and would not do, especially if she was out of sorts.

Rose was shooed out of the annexe from under her mum's feet and walked along the lane towards the Captain's House. She dawdled along the road, looking at the water running down the gully at the edges of the tarmac, wondering if the heavy rain that woke her last night had damaged anything. A toot of a horn and whistle made her turn. She turned around and she saw a large white van coming down the lane towards her. The window was down. She could see a muscular tanned arm sticking out. Then a head appeared and, as the van got closer, she saw a large infectious grin plastered across the face with eyes that twinkled with humour.

"You must be the lovely Rose that has gotten herself the Captain's House. Everyone is talking about you in the pub, but we have never seen you. Would you like a lift, or shall I meet you there?"

Rose giggled and retorted, "As there is only about 50 metres left to walk, I will decline the lift." Then she added, "My mum told me never to talk to strangers or accept a lift from someone I don't know!"

As the van passed her, Rose noticed that the property maintenance company logo was plastered all over the side of the van. She did not notice this when speaking to the driver as she was caught up in his mischievous patter. She found herself walking faster, practically trotting along the road in her haste to meet him at the house. She was drawn to his easy-going smile and was hoping that his business acumen was as good as his looks.

Steve was waiting for her in the garden but had wasted no time. He had taken a picture of the chimney stack on his smart phone and was preparing to send it on to a colleague for his views. "I reckon that is your first job and maybe the most expensive, along with the roof and other structural problems, but it is all do-able."

Looking across at Rose, standing with her arms crossed and legs astride in a classical defensive position, he said, "I am sure we can work something out. How about you show me around the house."

Rose unlocked the front door and stood aside to let Steve wander about the house by himself. He was wearing jeans and a grey polo shirt with his business logo on the back. He seemed to take over the space and once again wasted no time taking more photographs, measurements, and other details to assist in his quotes.

As he came downstairs and faced her again in the hallway, he said, "Well, I need some time to come up with some figures for you, but if you want my honest opinion – it will be costly." He smiled reassuringly and patted her arm gently. "I know I am supposed to be very businesslike and give you a cost which gives me a large profit, but truth is I would love to make this house nice again. With the added bonus of getting to know you."

Rose shifted from side to side nervously and then jumped from a clatter from the back of the house. They both rushed into the living room and there, in the middle of the room, surrounded by dust motes rising in the morning sunshine, was the Captain's hat. It had fallen from the mantelpiece where her dad had carefully placed it a few days earlier.

Rose wondered if the Captain agreed with her gut feeling of Steve. Could he help her restore the house to its original splendour or was the Captain warning her that he was out to take her for a ride? Rose bent down and picked the hat up and put it on the window seat. Placing it right at the back in the corner. She sighed quietly to herself.

Fourteen

Rose left Steve wandering around the outside of the Captain's House, making notes and putting together an action plan and a list of contractors that he would need to work with to complete a quote for Rose. She had to get back to the annexe to say farewell to her mum and thank her for her time and advice over the last few weeks. Her mum was quite prepared to stay for a further few weeks and Val was more than happy to have her stay, but Rose wanted to be by herself in order to work things out in her head. If she was at work, she would have tackled the whole thing like a project, with timelines and targets, and she was starting to think, after meeting Steve and seeing him making lists and plans, that she should do likewise. It was her house and her money after all.

Her dad arrived promptly mid-afternoon and whisked her mum away, promising her a romantic meal for two on the way home as he had missed her. Rose rather suspected that he had a pile of dirty washing and had missed her mum's home cooking more. She looked around the annexe, looking for something to do to keep herself busy and found that her mum had done all her washing and ironing. There was not a cushion out of place on the sofa. There was also a hotpot simmering in the oven that smelt divine.

Rose was tucking into her dinner when there was a knock on the internal door in the annexe. Rose opened the door to find Val with a large box of chocolates under her arm and a bottle of wine, with two glasses in her hands.

"Thought you might be missing your mum. Do you want some company?" Rose really wanted to spend the evening on her own, but decided it was churlish to turn Val away. She opened the door wide and stepped back and invited Val into the main room of the annexe.

"I am still eating my dinner, but chocolates are always welcome for pudding!"

It turned out that although Val was keen to keep Rose company, she was even keener to find out how she got on with Steve. Rose was tempted to tell Val that she did not like Steve, just to see her reaction, but her better self intervened. She told Val the truth. "I am sure that Steve would be the right person to help me with the house and he was quite nice to look at as well."

Val and Rose polished off the box of chocolates and the bottle of wine, tittering like a couple of teenagers about men until it was very late.

The following day was wet and windy and Rose did not venture out. The rain was coming down hard and fast and the ground was awash with surface water. Rose spent the day with her laptop open on her lap and made her own lists of jobs, tasks, and the all-important wish list of the Captain's House. She needed to search all the rooms thoroughly in the house before any building work took place. Most of the soft furnishings in the house would need to be taken down and either thrown away and replaced or cleaned and restored. Rose wondered if there was anything hidden in the lumpy mattress after all, as her mum had teased. She loved the rose design in the bedroom and wasted most of the afternoon on the web, looking at the modern equivalent in duvets, cushions, and curtains. Her mum had suggested that she put the white kitchen goods, washing machine, freezer etc. in the nearest outbuilding, so she could keep the beautiful, if old-fashioned kitchen cupboards that were built into the walls of the house. Rose added 'explore the outbuildings' to her to-do list on the computer and wondered where Christian slept during the winter months. She did not want to inadvertently upset the man by prying or disturbing his belongings that could be stored somewhere on her property. Rose decided to explore the village and try and find Christian to make sure he did not have anything hidden in the buildings.

Rose caught up with Christian a few days later, dozing on the sea wall. He was lying length-ways along the wall and from his relaxed position he resembled a lazy cat stretched out in the warmth of the sunshine. She sat down next to him and whispered quietly, "You look comfortable." Christian opened one eye languidly and slowly sat up.

"You are the lady from the Captain's House, how is it going up there?"

Rose told Christian about all her plans for the house and what her plans were for the nearest outbuilding. Rose asked him directly, "Are you keeping anything at the house?" but appeased him by telling him, "You are welcome to keep stuff up there, but you need to tell me where and what it is so that I know that it is yours."

Christian was chuffed to bits that Rose trusted him, despite his appearance and different way of life. It was a refreshing change that someone would take him seriously.

"I will help you as much as I can if you are planning to make the house your home. I can help you find out more about your mysterious Captain," he joked.

Christian was tempted to tell her more about himself and why he was sleeping rough at all, but his natural shyness stopped him. Rose walked along the shoreline with Christian, just casually talking about the house. She found him surprisingly easy to talk to. They finished up sharing a bag of chips.

Christian remarked as Rose was leaving, "I promise to come up to the Captain's House very soon and share some secrets of the house and the Captain with you."

Rose wanted to insist that they returned to the house straight away and was tempted to bundle him into the car, like the cops do on the television. But she knew in her heart of hearts that if she did, that he would clam up and certainly not appreciate the lift or the interference. All good things come to those who wait, but what did the Captain's House have in store for her?

It was mid-afternoon when Rose wandered into the second-hand bookstore and antique shop alongside the harbour. There was something about a second-hand bookshop that she could not resist. The smell of the old, decaying books and the slight mustiness to the air was like an exotic fragrance to a bookworm like herself and she took a deep breath and a long sniff in appreciation. The man sitting behind the till looked up from the book he was reading and grinned knowingly back at her, returning her wide smile with one of his own.

Rose clutched her bag closer to her chest and moved along the narrow aisle, trying to avoid the oversized books that were displayed at the front of the shop. She came to an abrupt halt in front of the antique section and carefully pulled out one of the books from the shelf. The book was a warm burgundy colour and the pages were brown and slightly rippled. It was an old family bible, quite small, but the price, lightly inscribed in faint pencil, was huge. She carefully placed in back into the shelf and stepped away.

The shop consisted of small rooms and tiny corridors connecting them. Each room contained hundreds of books in floor to ceiling shelving and some in stacks on the floor. Each section was labelled, and Rose searched for the 'maritime section'. There were books on all kinds of boats and ships from practical manuals of sailing to maritime law and accounts of naval captains. She picked out armfuls and made her way back to the counter to pay for them.

The man smiled and greeted Rose. "How lovely to see that you have found what you were looking for. Pop them down here and I will find you a bag to put them in. They won't fit in that silly bag you are holding."

She laughed and looked at her handbag. "You are so right. I was not going to buy anything. I only came in to have a look around and now look at me," she retorted. "I don't know anything about anything nautical and I really want to learn. I am sure my house used to belong to a sailor or Captain or something, so I need to get on board! So to speak."

"You need to pop into the antique section then while you are here," he said, "there is plenty of nautical rubbish to be found in there. Some of it is modern nautical rubbish to be honest, but just tell Geoff I sent you and he will make sure that what you buy is a genuine antique if you find something."

"I am not looking at buying anything, but there again I was not looking at buying any books when I came in here. I will be back again I am sure, now I know you are here. You can't keep me away from a bookshop for long. How much do I owe you?"

"Twenty pounds for that little lot I am afraid, but I have thrown in a jute bag with the shop's logo on, so you can find us again." He pointed at the shop's logo and at the address printed below it. The website address was listed as well.

"You will definitely see me again, I am sure," Rose said as she made her way back down the narrow aisle and ducked into the room on the right that she had missed earlier. There were several customers already in the shop and the small space was even smaller and harder to navigate. Rose sneaked past an older lady wearing a smart navy-blue business suit and crept up the stairs, following a faded paper stuck to the plasterboard with a yellowing piece of sellotape.

At the top of the stairs, her mouth fell open with surprise. There were glass cabinets in this side of the building, not the bookshelves that were 'next door', but they were crammed with all manner of odd objects, china, guns, swords, and teddies. All the cabinets were numbered and appeared to be locked. She stood very still and cast her eyes around the room, trying to take it all in. Her eyes swept over the organized chaos in some of the cabinets and she edged closer to have a look at the collection of teddies that were the only things that were displayed in an orderly fashion. Side by side they sat. In solid, straight lines, their backs ramrod straight, and their heads set very straight on their furry bodies. All their eyes faced front and they looked straight at her, so straight! She mirrored their stance and felt like a child again, looking for the one with the crooked nose or the wonky ear. Rose did not like perfect, she liked a bit of character. She was sure that this was why she was drawn to her old house, as her house certainly did not lack that.

Next to the teddies were all manner of weapons, jumbled together in an appealing mess. The labels that were loosely tied to each object were tangled too. There were old guns, shotguns and rifles all pointing in random directions. At the back of the cabinets were a couple of old swords, propped up and leaning against the back of the frame.

Next to the cabinets in front of the window was an old writing desk, and in the groove at the back of the desk next to the ink well was a long black cylinder with a brass top. As Rose moved to reached across the desk to pick it up, a shrill voice pierced the silence, "Do you want to look at that? Shall I get it for you?"

Rose jumped and spun around and came face to face with the lady that she had squeezed pass downstairs.

"I have been watching you on the CCTV screens, I am sorry I startled you, but you have been staring at the telescope for about five minutes now I wanted to make sure you were OK."

Rose was certain that she had just moved across from the teddy cabinet just seconds ago, but this lady seemed sure that five minutes had passed. Rose peered at the face of the lady, trying to make sense of it all and all her features blended into one. Her face faded slowly. She could hear a bell ringing and the sounds of the sea. The waves crashing and bellowing. Then there was a blackness then a light grey and slowly, very slowly, the face came into view again.

The eyes in the face looked concerned and serious and a glass of water was thrust under her nose.

"Drink a sip of that, my dear, you must have passed out. You were lucky I caught you, sweetie. If you had fallen an inch either way you would have caused a tremendous calamity, brought down one of the cabinets on to your head and the wrath of Geoff, the owner of this place. Not to mention how much it would of cost you if the contents were broken and damaged."

Rose did as she was asked and took small sips of water and lowered herself to the floor gingerly. The floor was smooth as the floorboards were worn, but the floor was not level, it sloped in every direction and sitting on the floor did not have the stablishing effect she was looking for.

"My name is Phyliss and I am the manager of this place, are you sure you are OK? I can call Mary, who helps on a Thursday, she is a retired nurse. She can take a look at you, if you like. Or do you think you need an ambulance? I read somewhere that you can faint if you have not had anything to eat. Now have you eaten today, sweetie? I have a box of doughnuts in the office, would you like one?"

Phyliss continued with her constant chatter, completely oblivious to the fact that Rose was not listening to her. She was not intentionally ignoring her, but her gaze had fallen on the telescope. It did not look like a telescope. It was a black cylinder and resembled an old tent peg or weight. It looked nothing like the ornate brass telescope that was fixed to the floor in the house.

She got up shakily and leaned heavily on the writing desk to help support her weight as she did so. The telescope rolled towards her and she caught it just before it rolled off the desk onto the floor. It was heavy. Very heavy. She had caught it with one hand and had to bring the other hand up very quickly to cradle the other side before she dropped it.

Phyliss, tapped her arm for attention and swung her around to face her. "You stay right here, young lady, I am making a nice cup of tea and I am going to ring Mary to have a look at you. One of those doughnuts has your name on it. Sit back down on the floor if you feel 'funny' again," she demanded.

Rose took her at her word and sat down, cradling the telescope in her arms as she did so. She could not resist peeking at the label as she did so. The telescope was over two hundred pounds, which she was in no position to spend, but she knew she had to have it. It was not the same feeling that she got when she was in a clothes shop and had to have a pair of shoes or a handbag to match something else. It was a gut feeling. A compelling, all-encompassing feeling that was making her feel quite ill. She was glad she was sitting down, albeit taking over the whole of the tiny floor of the room with her legs stretched out in front of her. She was glad she was the only customer in the shop. It would be embarrassing if people had to step over her or there were more than one Phyliss fussing over her.

Phyliss returned with a bone china cup and saucer and a matching tea plate with a jam doughnut. She took one look at Rose on the floor and clambered down to the floor beside her. She passed her the cup and saucer and watched silently as Rose sipped the warm sweet tea. When she had finished her tea, Phyliss exchanged the cup and saucer for the tea plate with the doughnut and waited till she had finished all of it and was wiping the stray crumbs and jam from her lips with the back of her hand.

Then the torrent of words started again. Phyliss was one of these ladies that genuinely cared for everyone she met. She had a warm, caring personality and made friends with everyone. Rose was no exception. Then she swept Rose off her feet with an embracing hug, miraculously managing to gather the cup, saucer, and plate as well. Together, they squeezed back down the stairs without getting wedged in the restricted space and Rose was gently pushed into a leather armchair behind the counter.

"I could not get Mary to pop in as there was no reply when I called, but the colour has come back to your cheeks and you look alright now. I want you to wait there awhile before I let you go home!"

"I am just fine now. I have taken enough of your time. I do feel very silly, what am I like."

To Rose's surprise the telescope was sitting in front of her on the desk. "Did you pick this up, Phyliss?" asked Rose.

"Oh yes, I could see that you had taken a fancy to it as you were cradling it like a baby. I assumed you wanted to buy it."

Rose and Phyliss bartered over the telescope and agreed a price. Phyliss carefully wrapped the telescope in bubble wrap for her to take home, adding her business card with a handwritten amendment on the back of her telephone number, just in case Rose needed her.

That night Rose fell asleep, surrounded by nautical books and the telescope beside her on the bed.

Fifteen

The next visit Rose made to the house was in her car and she
had to squeeze out of the car and step immediately into the
wilderness of a garden. There was just a very small cobbled area to
the side of the house, which was suitable for parking and was
loosely referred as the 'drive'. The neglected shrubs were hanging
over the cobbles, bedraggled by the wind and rain, leaves turned
black from the winter's frost. As the weather had been wet for a
few days, her clothes got soaked and her trainers were muddy
before she had gone anywhere. Although, she did notice that there
was a Steve shape in the largest bush, where he had got in and out
of his van earlier.

She was happy for Steve to visit on his own to assess the work
that needed to be done, but she did not let him have her keys just yet.
She trusted him, but she had not explored every room in the property
carefully and this was the reason for her visit today.

She let herself in with her key and checked that the Captain's hat
was still on the window seat overlooking the river. She could not help
but look for the handsome man that she saw when she first visited
the house and was undecided whether to keep the house or not. She
did not see anyone from the window, but she sat down next to the
hat and leaned against the wall, resting her head against the smooth
wood that surrounded the window. The sun rays warmed her
through the glass, and she felt warm and contented.

She found herself daydreaming about the mystery man that she had glimpsed walking along the footpath and wondered why she had not seen him around the village as she had been staying at Little Lanterns for a while now. She smiled. She had only mentioned him to Lisa, but she had not mentioned him to anyone else, even her mum. Perhaps she had imagined him, and he was the ideal excuse for keeping the house. The perfect man. Rose knew perfectly well that this did not exist, but it was nice to think that everyone had a soulmate and hers was just out there waiting to meet her. Rose was drawn to Steve too. She knew that she admired his practical skills and his canny sense of humour. He was not an unattractive man. Rose hoped that he would be a good friend and confidante. She could certainly use a few.

Rose ran her hands across the back of the window seat and her fingers were stalled as she encountered an uneven surface with deep grooves. She looked closer and it looked like there were marks of some kind carved into the wood. They were tiny. Rose could not decipher the markings. She would need a magnifying glass. She looked for more marks around the window seat and in the surrounding wood and was disappointed when she could not find any more.

She paced around the room examining all the surfaces and tapping her feet on the floorboards, like she had seen people do on the TV, waiting for a loose floorboard to produce a treasure map or a handful of gold coins. To her eternal shame, as she was tip-tapping on the floor like a demented dancer from 'River Dance', who should stroll in but Steve.

"Is everything all right?" he demanded as he dashed in. "I thought the door had slammed shut. You were trapped and tapping for attention."

"I think I would have yelled help first," retorted Rose. She explained what she was doing and shared the joke with Steve. She did not mention the strange marks she had found.

She was not expecting Steve at the house and wondered why he had stopped by. "I was just on my way to Little Lanterns, to drop the quote in your letter box. I saw your car parked up at the house."

Steve went on, "I am an old-fashioned guy and prefer to print a quote as well as send an e-mail that most people print out anyway." He sheepishly admitted, "I was also looking for an excuse to bump into you."

He stared at his boots and muttered quietly, "Would you like to visit the local pub with me this evening for dinner and listen to some local lads in a band afterwards?"

Rose knew that for all his bluster he was embarrassed. "That is a great idea, we can discuss the house as we eat."

Steve left the envelope with her. "I will pick you up from Little Lanterns at seven this evening," he promised.

Rose put the envelope in the back pocket of her jeans and continued her exploration of the house. Rose did not often procrastinate, but she did not want to open the envelope while she was in the house. She wanted her time to be positive in the house and did not want to be counting her pennies and worrying about where it was all coming from. She grabbed her phone and took a photograph of the carvings, she sat on the stairs and did her best to enlarge them. It did not work. The carving became out of focus and blurry each time she enhanced the image. Rose wondered if Val had a magnifying glass she could borrow.

She sat on the stairs and felt the rustle of the envelope in her back pocket and sighed softly to herself. She knew she had a ready pot of money to play with. She just had to budget to make sure it lasted. She was sure that Steve would do all he could to help and found herself strangely looking forward to meeting him later. It was time to start mending the house for her Captain and unravelling all the mysteries within.

Sixteen

R ose felt like a teenager again as she was getting ready to go out for dinner with Steve. She had ransacked her bedroom and her suitcases were upended at the foot of the bed. Clothes were strewn all over the bed and floor and all the doors were open with hangers displaying different outfits and accompanying accessories. The radio was playing loudly in the background, belting out the latest hits. Rose hummed away to the tune and tapped the beat out with her hand on the pine dressing table as she surveyed the mess. Glancing at the large clock in the hallway reflected in the mirror of the dressing table, she realised she was running late.

She knew she liked Steve but did not want to give him the wrong impression, so she tucked the LBD, her little slinky black dress back into the wardrobe. She looked at her smart skirt and flowery shirt and decided it was too 'office and work' like. She then looked at her smart black jeans and bright orange silk shirt. A fitted black jacket and the ensemble was ready. She was just zipping her feet into her smart suede black boots when she heard a knock at the door. She hurried out of the bedroom, shutting the door on the chaos within.

It was not Steve; the knocking was coming from the internal door. So, she changed direction and opened the right door. Val noticed she was getting ready to go out and handed her the magnifying glass that she had asked for earlier and left her to it with smug grin. There was more knocking. This time coming from the external door and Rose took a deep breath and opened the door to Steve.

Steve stood in the doorway, made his apologies for being early, and then asked her, "Would you explain why you are taking a magnifying glass out with you? What have you heard about me?" Working out his saucy intonations, she blushed a deep crimson colour and it was her turn to look at her feet.

Steve had not brought his van to take her out. He also owned an old Triumph Herald Convertible and she clambered into the front seat and inhaled the scent of polish and leather. He had also added a new air freshener, hanging from the rear-view mirror. It was obvious that Steve had recently tidied the car and a quick peek into the back seat confirmed this. There was a heap of old magazines and sweet wrappers that had been shoved onto the back seat as he had tidied the rest of the car. Typical man! It did not take long to drive to the pub and Steve did his best to put her at ease, as he could sense her nerves. He explained that the locals were a friendly bunch, and the band was made up of his old school friends, George and James. They also worked with him from time to time, as George was a plumber and James an electrician.

The pub was set back from the road, with a large forecourt which doubled as a car park. The pub had lamps in every window and emitted an inviting glow. Bob and Doreen, the publicans, were introduced to Rose when they arrived at the long narrow bar, which ran the length of the pub. They were delighted to meet the new owner of the Captain's House and Doreen showed the pair of them to a table in the window. Rose found herself hiding behind the large menu that Doreen had given her, so she did not have to face Steve. She was not normally shy and nervous, but she felt like the new girl at school on her first day and had a date to deal with all at the same time. They ordered dinner and then Steve gently took the menu out of her hand and pointed out, "As I am taking you out for your dinner, I would like to look at you!"

Rose quickly changed the subject from looking at each other, "Shall we talk about the quote?"

They both adjusted their positions in their chairs and assumed a more business-like pose subconsciously. Rose explained, "I am happy with the quote," but, remembering her dad's advice just in time, she added, "it was just a bit more than I was expecting," with a shy smile. Steve went very quiet and Rose instantly regretted her choice of words.

They then discussed the old house in a little more detail. Steve was on her wave length and seemed to know what she wanted before she had even processed the thoughts. Rose was sure that he would enjoy working on the house as much as she would and threw caution into the wind.

"I would love you to take on my house and help me make it into a home. Perhaps we should set a date?" she replied tentatively.

"I have some work on now that is keeping me busy, but it should not take long to finish up and I will be over at your house before you know it!" Steve vowed to work like a demented Trojan to get the work done. He was keen to start on the house and liked to see a smile on Rose's face.

The arrival of their food and the fact that the business decision was now out of the way made Rose's shyness disappear. Rose found that she could talk to Steve and really enjoyed his company. While they ate, Rose watched George, James, and the other guys from the band set up their instruments, amplifiers, and speakers at the other end of the pub. While they did not interrupt Rose and Steve's dinner, they kept a constant eye on them.

When they had finished their meal, out of the corner of her eye, Rose glimpsed an old painting hanging on the wall depicting the Captain's House, surrounded by a cottage garden in full bloom. A woman's head could be seen amongst the flowers. Rose got up and went to examine it closely. It was her Captain's house in the background, but the painter's emphasis was clearly the garden and the lady.

An elderly gentleman seated at the bar, with a brown and white spaniel at his feet, said, "Yes, my dear. That is your house, many years ago. The painting is one of many that the old Captain swore he had painted himself. It is rumoured that it was given to the pub in lieu of his bar bill! My name is Mickey and this little fella," as he bent down and stroked the spaniel's silky ears, "is my best friend Bert."

"I have seen you walking on the footpath that runs past my house on the other side of the river," Rose replied.

Steve then appeared at her side and admonished Mickey in a good-natured way, "You? Stealing my dinner date?" he chuckled.

Seventeen

The band were very good. George and James threw in a couple of romantic numbers to their set and, with a glance over to Steve and Rose, they announced, "Now it's time to get everyone in the mood for love ..." They finished off the set with a lively rock and roll number. While they were packing away afterwards, Steve and Rose joined them. Steve told them that Rose was letting them work on the house, so they needed to finish the job they were all working on post haste.

"Yay," grinned George, "I am looking forward to working on the infamous Captain's House." James, however, looked very worried.

"You do know that the house has a reputation for being haunted? Oooh I am not sure about working there."

"Hey, my Captain is friendly, I'm sure, but I still have loads to find out about him and that lady over there in the painting of the garden that I glimpsed just now."

They all walked across to the painting and Rose pointed out the lady and they all agreed that there was a lady in the painting that no one but Rose had spotted before.

"Whoa," said James, "how spooky, that you of all people, the new owner of the house, spotted her. No one else has noticed her before, we all thought her head was a big flower!"

"Oh, you big girl's blouse and big coward," accused Steve immediately. "I would work anywhere if I got paid and working in a haunted house adds extra excitement and a pretty face around the place works for me. Rose and the spooky lady in the garden works for me too!" he added cheekily.

"The more money I earn, the more in the kitty for my new place. I need space, so I can make as much noise and mess as I like, and no one will mind!" James concluded.

Rose feared for his prospective neighbours, as he was the drummer in the band. Steve and Rose were the last to leave and the bar and dining area were clean and the last of the washed glasses were being put away as Rose called goodnight to Doreen. Doreen called across, "You should pop over for a coffee one day soon as I'm sure there might be some more of the Captain's paintings in the loft." She added that if Rose asked Bob to look for them, he might do it. "If I ask him, I will still be waiting at Christmas. The paintings were not all of the house, I am sure that there is one of a ship."

Rose chattered excitedly to Steve all the way home in the car about the paintings and the lady. She was sure that other painting was of the Captain's actual ship and was only brought back to reality when Steve switched the engine off. He leaned across to her and kissed her cheek saying, "Thank you for a lovely evening," before she had time to engage her brain. She sat stunned. She then leaned across and returned the kiss, only this time he had moved his head and she kissed him squarely on the lips. She giggled and grinned at Steve. He laughed with her and promised to call her soon as she climbed out of the car.

She turned back and wondered if she should ask him in for coffee, but there was a little toot from the Herald's horn and Steve was heading out of the driveway into the lane. She inserted her key into the lock and leaned against the door. Her thoughts were scrambled, and she was not sure what to make of the evening or her feelings for Steve.

She put the kettle on and made a cup of tea and laid out the plans of the Captain's House on the table. She looked at the house, the boundaries, and the footpath. She thought about the lady in the painting and wondered if she was the Captain's wife or lover. Was the bench made for her? She could not remember if she saw the bench in the painting. If it was, it was not in the foreground, but in amongst the flowers or next to the front door. Perhaps it sat at the rear of the garden overlooking the river, footpath, and the sea in the distance.

Rose put her elbows on the table and looked again at the outbuildings marked on the drawings, perhaps one used to be a stable and maybe the one that was close to the river was a boat house. The river was only wide enough for a rowing boat, but that would be a quick way to get to the sea as well as the footpath. She imagined herself wandering around the garden in bloom and sitting on the bench. She fell asleep at the table with her head in her arms. She woke up as the dawn broke, tired and very stiff from sleeping at the table all night. Her arm was resting on the plans and her index fingers were pointing at the footpath. Her mystery man popped into her thoughts and she attempted to remember her dream. Her finger traced the footpath.

Rose got up from the table, groaning as her muscles signaled their protest. She made herself another cup of tea and prepared to go to bed for a proper sleep. She fell into a deep sleep and did not wake until eleven. She had six texts on her mobile and two missed calls. Three were from her mum and two were from Steve and the most recent was from Mike. Mike had been completely forgotten about the night before and Rose felt uneasy that she had almost invited Steve in for coffee! Mike was letting her know that he was having a good time and she should have come with him and taken him up on his offer.

Should she still wish to invest, the time was now. He wanted to know if she had given up on her house yet. If she had given up as expected, she was to call him. He would give her a second chance!

Rose then read Steve's texts which were completely different. They thanked her for last night and asked her if she would like to do it again sometime. His second text was very businesslike and suggested a date for starting on the Captain's House and perhaps a preliminary meeting to discuss the schedule of work. Rose was pleased that he was attempting to keep things separate and decided that she would like to meet him again, both socially and to work on her house. Steve was a breath of fresh air in comparison to Mike and her mystery man was just as much a mystery to her as the Captain. She was going to spend the next few weeks until work could start on the house finding her Captain and looking for more clues in the house.

Eighteen

Rose knew she would have to be more methodical in searching the house for more clues about the Captain and decided that she would need another critical eye to help. Her first thought was Steve, but he was anxious to finish his current work to start on the Captain's House. He was a nonstarter. Her mum could be extremely critical, normally when she did not want her to be. Her dad would look at the structure of the property and had already made himself useful when he visited. Rose had only sent brief text messages to her best friend, Lisa. She had not invited her down to see the house. Rose knew that she had wanted to make a start on the house. She wanted to impress her friend with her progress and secretly make her a bit jealous. This was not to be. Rose needed Lisa to help her look for clues and she valued her opinion, even if it could be a bit harsh sometimes.

It did not take much persuading and the arrangements were made for Lisa to come down the next weekend. Lisa was very keen to share her house. Rose was sick of writing lists, making notes, and just wandering around dreaming. It was time to take her head out of the clouds and stop making excuses.

Rose visited the house every day that week and explored every nook and cranny. She resisted taking the Captain's hat and coat back to the annexe, as she was sure that they should always stay in the house. She did not find any more carvings, just a lot of dust and debris in the cupboards. She took the curtains down from all the rooms. They were very threadbare, smelly, and slightly damp. Rose was not sure if they would survive the washing machine. She could have the patterns and colours copied and new curtains made. The beautiful bedspread that was left on the double bed was equally fragile and she folded it up carefully and added to the pile of odds and ends from the house. The mattress was large, lumpy, and smelly. It would be a two-man job to get it down the stairs, so she decided to wait for either Lisa or Steve to give her a hand. It needed to be thrown away and she did not want to leave it in the garden. Perhaps she would ask Steve to take it away in his van. When she spoke with her mum to tell her of her progress, her mum reminded her to split it open as that was where people used to hide their money and valuables. Rose appeased her mum by agreeing to do this, but inwardly cringed at her mum's stupidity. She thought she might have the last laugh when there was nothing there but springs and whatever the stuffing was made of. She suspected horsehair as the smell of it reminded her of a musty stable.

The old iron bedstead looked forlorn standing in the middle to the room. The only other furniture in the room was the old chair with the Captain's coat hanging off the wing. The windows were exceptionally long in this room, from floor to ceiling. The coat was clearly visible in its entirety to walkers on the footpath and from the lane. Was the Captain's ghost just an old coat after all? But there was an all-prevailing smell of tobacco in the bedroom and the coat just reeked of the stuff.

She found an old broom and finally felt like the lady of the house, sweeping the floorboards clean and creating a fine sheen of dust everywhere. Downstairs, the old armchair was moved from the hallway back into the living room and in front of the fire at an angle to catch the view as well. She gave all the windows a quick wash, being very careful with the stained-glass windows as they looked fragile and the wooden frames appeared rotten.

The only room she gave a wide berth was the smelly bathroom. The toilet had been cleaned by her mum who was caught short on her first visit to the house and had to use it. She had returned with a vengeance and cleaned the toilet thoroughly. She had even placed a plastic air fresher with a rose fragrance on the floor next to the toilet bowl. Her mum's idea of a joke. The toilet was an old-fashioned one with an overhead cistern and a metal chain hanging down. There was black and white tiling everywhere. The white tiles had a greyish tinge to them. The smell was off putting. Rose only went into the bathroom if she needed to.

The house was looking as ship shape as possible with a minimum amount of furniture. It still seemed to retain the spirit of the Captain and it resembled a boat more than ever. As the interior was just a shell it contrasted vehemently with the garden and landscape outside. It drew Rose's attention to the wilderness of the garden. The garden seemed to be vying for attention as well as all manner of shrubs and trees that knocked against the fragile windowpanes whenever there was the slightest breeze.

Rose still had to explore the outhouses, but decided to tackle these buildings when Lisa got there. She needed to remember not to throw anything away until she checked with Christian that whatever it was did not belong to him. She wondered what Lisa would make of him and felt in her pocket for her mobile phone. She had not forgotten Val's advice of always bringing it to the house in case of an emergency.

Later that evening, she was soaking in a bath that was too hot and turning her a lobster pink when she realised that she had not made a reservation for dinner at the pub for that weekend. She promised Lisa faithfully that she would let her taste the local night life. She rolled her eyes towards the heavens as she imagined her friend's face when she was chatted up by Mickey and his dog, Bert, at the bar. She reached across the sides of the bath to grab her phone which was perched on a stack of toilet rolls on the windowsill. She wiped her hands on the soft towel that was hanging down from the sink next to her and dialed the pub. Doreen answered the phone just as the answerphone was cutting in. Her voice was shrill and loud. Rose made the reservation for dinner, but did not have to give her name as Doreen had recognised her voice. She implored Rose to pop down to the pub very soon as she had found something very interesting in the pub's attic.

Nineteen

Rose could not wait to visit the pub at the weekend with Lisa and she got up earlier than usual for her new 'lady of leisure' self and made herself a quick breakfast. She glanced at the messy rooms and resolved to tidy the annexe when she got back and to put some washing on, so the annexe was as tidy as the Captain's House. She had not seen Val for a few days, so she made her way round to the front of the main building and found Val on her hands and knees in the front driveway, knee deep in spring bedding plants and pots. There was all manner of spring flowers ready to go into the pots, from primulas to daffodils in their black shiny trays from the local garden centre. Val explained, "I need to keep the front of the house welcoming. Do you want a few plants for the Little Lantern's doorstep?"

Rose was delighted, "That would be lovely. Could I have a couple, one for each side and one of these brown pots for them to go into? I am sure I have seen some pots like that, stacked up in the Captain's garden." Val gave Rose a couple of trays of plants for the Captain's House.

She said, "You must brighten up the old place, even though it looks like it will fall down, with that wonky chimney."

Val was interested to hear that Doreen had found something in the attic of the pub but insisted on giving Rose the run down on Doreen. It appeared that there had been a disagreement many years before between Val and Doreen and there was not much of their old friendship left. Rose had never heard Val be so bitchy about anyone before, so it challenged her preconceptions of Val as well as her first impressions of Doreen.

"Don't you trust that Doreen," Val warned with an angry glare, "take what she says with a pinch of salt."

Unperturbed by this turn of conversation, Rose drove down to the pub and parked up in the forecourt, where Steve had parked. She had not noticed what the pub was called when she was out with Steve before, but hanging from the wall was a traditional pub sign which depicted several shipping vessels in a modern trendy design dictated by the local brewery. It was ironic that the pub was called 'The Ship'.

She walked from the bright sunshine into the darkened bar area and met Doreen wiping and dusting all the tables in the eating area and replacing the tatty bar mats with new ones, with the image of the sign hanging at the front.

"Oh, an excuse to sit down and stop working for a while," Doreen sighed as she sat down at the nearest table. "Do sit down with me and I will get Bob to go and get what we found."

At that point, she turned to the bar and yelled into thin air, "Rose is here, will you get what we have found? Keep the blanket over it as I want it to be a surprise."

Rose sat down with Doreen at the table and leant on the tabletop with her elbows. Bob appeared with what looked like a heavy painting. He could hardly lift it and he dragged one corner of it on the floor. This prompted another loud bellow from Doreen, "Do be careful with that, you don't want to damage it, Bob." Bob set it down in front of Rose and Doreen jumped up and whipped the blanket from the painting with a dramatic flourish.

There in front of Rose was the original pub sign which was of a large ship. It was a beautiful ship and it was sailing on calm blue sea. Rose recognised this ship but could not place it at first. Then the realisation dawned on her, it was the ship from her Captain's stained-glass windows in the house. The hallway and landing windows. There was no lighthouse, but the ship was so similar it was uncanny. Now, Rose wondered two things. Did the ship belong to the Captain or was the Captain so fond of a drink that he wanted to replicate the local pub's sign in his own home? Rose hoped it was the former.

Rose wanted to know why Doreen was sure she would have liked it. The stained windows at the house were small and intimate. They could not be seen from the lane and you had to be inside the house to really appreciate them. How did Doreen know that the ship was the same? How was Doreen acquainted with the house? Two big questions that started to worry Rose.

Bob and Doreen were both watching for the expression on her face when she looked across at them moments later. Rose was on her guard and kept her facial expressions as neutral as she could.

"Have you found my Captain's ship to match my house?" she found herself saying out loud.

Doreen replied, "I do hope so, it seemed to be painted in the same style as the painting over there."

She pointed over to the painting of the Captain's garden that had caught Rose's eye when she was out for dinner with Steve.

Rose was still not sure that Doreen was hiding anything from her so decided not to mention the comparison with the windows themselves.

"Can I take a photo of the sign with my phone?" she asked. "I could enlarge it and make it into a picture for my house. It would certainly fit in."

Doreen and Bob seemed to pause for a while before answering.

Then Doreen gestured with her hands, "Yes, take the photo now with your smartphone and come back another time with a better camera."

She explained that she was going to leave it on display for the locals to see for a while. Rose was looking forward to coming back and hoped to catch Mickey at the bar to see what he thought of the old sign and if he could remember it hanging at the front of the pub.

Twenty

After a short chat and coffee with Doreen and Bob, Rose made her escape and drove quietly back up the lane and parked up at the Captain's House. She paced around the side of the house and looked up at the windows to see if she could make out the ship beyond the hedge. You could see there was a ship in the window, but the finer detail could only be seen from inside the house, when the light shines through the window from outside. One of the secrets of the house. Rose had not lived in the house yet and it had been a while since there had been lights on inside the house. She was uneasy when she thought of Doreen. Doreen had not mentioned that she had ever visited the Captain's House and she knew from Val that Doreen and Bob had only had the pub for the last five years or so.

So many unanswered questions.

Doreen was not telling her the whole truth and for the first time since she arrived in the village, she had met someone who was not happy at her good fortune. Maybe Doreen liked the house and was waiting for it to come up for sale. She may have been disappointed when she found out that someone had inherited the house, wanted to keep it and not put it up for sale. Doreen had mentioned that she had some more paintings of the house, but she had only shown her the pub sign of the ship, while pointing out the similarities with the garden picture. Was there more she was not telling her? Her mind whirled as she tried to keep up with the many thoughts that were running through it. None of the scenarios that she pondered were nice and almost all had a sinister and threating notion. Doreen was all sweetness and light on the surface, but Rose was very perturbed at what might be lying beneath.

Rose wandered around the garden some more and found the pots that she had remembered in a heap by the old bench, which was once more toppled over and leaning on its back. She righted the bench and sat down on it and looked across at the unruly garden with its wild feel. She looked back at the front porch and saw the ideal place for her new pots. She had not swept the front porch in her previous cleaning frenzy and she pictured the porch freshly swept with pots of daffodils either side.

She could hear her dad's voice admonishing her for adding the finishing touches before the important primary building work had taken place. In her eyes, the wonky chimney added charm and the cottage would look even more charming with the flowerpots right there. If the chimney stack did not fall in the meantime. She thought that Steve would find the pots amusing too on his next visit.

Steve would be able to fill her in on Doreen and Bob, but she did not want him to think she was too nosey. She would have to be subtle and probe him in an unassuming manner. She was sure that Val would spill more beans without much prompting as well. It was disappointing that Rose did not feel as comfortable in the village as she used to, but Lisa was arriving at the weekend and Rose felt she could use a fresh approach. They had a meal booked at the pub, so they did not need to make an excuse to go and she would take her camera with her to take a decent shot of the sign. Lisa could ask Doreen about the other paintings kept in her attic, which Rose would feel uncomfortable about.

Rose popped into the house to check all was OK and to retrieve the broom to sweep the front porch in preparation for the daffodils. She noticed that the front doorstep was worn and the tiling that led from the step seemed to run into the front grass. She kicked the edge of the grass with her boots and scraped away the roots. The tiling continued into the grass. Rose had discovered what looked like the path through the garden and towards the front gate. It could not be a straight path, but Rose liked this as it seemed to match the rest of the house. Slightly wonky. She was very tempted to continue kicking and scraping the grass with her foot, but she seemed to be making a mess. She needed the right tools for the job and the ground needed to be slightly drier.

That was another job that could be tackled as the seasons changed. Finding the path would not take long and it would be very satisfying. You could just follow the path and see where it leads, just like that 'Time Team' on the telly. It was sure to lead to the gate, but the whole process would define the shape of the garden. Rose would need to take a closer look at the painting in the pub to see if there were any more clues.

Her mood had lifted and when she left the house after checking it was all secure again, she found herself singing to the radio in the minutes it took to drive back to the annexe. When she sat down again, she found her thoughts returning to the peculiar visit to the pub that morning and all the emotion that it had created. She grabbed her laptop and went straight back on to the maritime site that she had previously been looking at.

Rose had no prior knowledge of ships or maritime history, but in no time at all she was out at sea. She was all at once lost in the details of square-rigged galleons to four-masted steel-hulled barques. The East India ships were easy to identify, and she found out that that captains of the East India ships had the highest status among merchant captains. Their crews had extra opportunities to bring home goods for private sale as well. She knew that the Captain that she thought belonged to her house was not of the right era for the ship depicted on the pub's sign. There must be a connection to the house, but what was it?

Twenty-One

Lisa called at half past seven on Saturday morning. She woke Rose who was still sleeping and expecting a call from Lisa at a more civilised hour or at least about lunchtime. Her mobile phone trilled and vibrated on her bedside table and interrupted her rather interesting dream about her mysterious stranger who just happened to be calling her to ask her out on at date. Rose answered the phone with a surprised husky whisper and was shocked to hear her friend's voice bellowing down the handset.

"Oh, were you asleep? Was so looking forward to seeing you and the house that I could not sleep, so thought that I would make an early start. Whoops, I'm here. Can you pick me up from the station, sweetheart?"

Rose sleepily agreed to pick Lisa up as soon as she was decent.

Lisa was astonished to see Rose pull up outside the station in record time, in just under half an hour. She piled into the car, dumping all her bags on the back seat. She looked as if she was staying for a month with all the bags she had with her, but, as they drove away, she confessed that she had been picking up some bits and pieces for Rose and her new home every time she went shopping. Lisa was born to shop and spent most of her time either on the Internet or in a shopping centre shopping. As Rose drove around the back streets of the town, seeking the road back to the village, Lisa cried, "Surely, we could catch a cup of coffee somewhere. I am parched." Rose chortled and caught her breath. As she coughed to clear her throat she announced, "that it was a lovely, fine day – too nice to spend shopping!"

Lisa gently touched her shoulder. "What seems to be the matter with you? No shopping on a Saturday morning, no coffee? Gosh, you are either getting old or been stuck in the country for far too long. Is the house so nice you are that desperate to show me?"

Rose carried on driving, looking straight ahead at the bus that was pulling out from a bus stop. She ignored these teasing comments and focused on the task of driving. Lisa then started to giggle, giggle, and then giggle some more. Lisa pulled out a comb that was stuck in the back of Rose's hair.

"My oh my. You came out with your comb still in your hair!"

Rose was mortified. She tried not to show it. Surely she would have felt the comb against her head. It was a small, black plastic one that had come free from the front of a magazine years ago. Lisa turned the comb over in her hands, running her fingers over the embossed 'Just Seventeen' logo. They shared this joke all the way back to the annexe, discussing the magazine in detail. The things they remembered, the articles and posters that they had cut out and stuck on their bedroom walls.

Lisa loved Little Lanterns but was cross that she was not driven to the Captain's House first. Rose pacified her by putting the kettle on and put a plate of pastries into the small oven to warm for breakfast. She dumped all Lisa's bags in the spare bedroom and started to feel and prod a few. Lisa was close behind and grabbed a few bags and took them out of the bedroom and shoved them on an armchair out of her reach. Only once the coffee was poured into a couple of chunky mugs, did Lisa allow Rose to look in the bags. Rose drew out a pair of cushions with a rose pattern and a lovely old jug that would look perfect on a windowsill in the house. There was a brass poker with a ship design for a handle in another bag. All in all, there were all the homely touches for the Captain's House displayed on the living room carpet. There was something for every room. It must have taken Lisa hours to search out all these goodies and Rose was touched by her friend's kindness.

The rose design seemed to be a feature of the Captain's House. After the girls had eaten every last crumb of the pastries, Rose showed Lisa the old curtains and bedspread from the house. The design was terribly similar.

"Wow, I only bought the cushions because your name was Rose. Oh, and of course, I liked them as well!" Lisa stated. Rose was taken aback by another similarity and the fact that indeed her name was Rose and the predominant design of all the soft furnishings that were left in the Captain's House were roses. How spooky.

Lisa loved the old furnishings and agreed that they should either get them restored or get them copied onto more modern fabric.

Lisa said, "Your Captain's House seems to like roses and I bet there are rose bushes in the garden. Seems like every Captain has a Rose!"

Rose found the cardboard box on the top of the wardrobe that she had brought the groceries from home and packed all her new bits and pieces into the box.

"I am very tempted to put these around the place on Steve's first day on the job. Together with the daffodil pots I am sure that will make him laugh."

Rose looked at Lisa's face. She had not told her about Steve. She took a deep breath and started to describe Steve in detail to her friend. She wondered what Lisa would make of him and whether she would berate her or be pleased that she had been out to dinner with him. Thank goodness she remembered before they went to the pub for dinner. Otherwise, someone else might have brought it up and Lisa would have never let her forget it.

Rose found that she had missed Lisa and her chatter, even her insufferable advice. She put the kettle on for the third time and said that they really should go to the Captain's House after this one.

Twenty-Two

Lisa wanted to know all the details about Steve and told her off for not telling her before now. Rose tried to pacify her with the fact that Steve would just be working on the house. Lisa reckoned that Steve would be working on her. The banter flew about between the two of them over their last cup of coffee and soon they began the short walk from the annexe to the Captain's House.

Rose needed some fresh air after the coffee that they had both drunk and the weather seemed to be set fair. They strode along the lane, in shirt sleeves holding their jumpers in their hands, in the warm spring sunshine. She paused at the gate which was the only gap in the hedge. It allowed her friend to drink in the view. Lisa was impressed by the silence of the countryside around them. Lisa said, "Complete silence, absolutely nothing. Total silence."

Rose told her, "Listen again, really listen. What silence are you raving about?"

They both stood together, listening hard. They could hear birdsong from the hedgerow and a faint snuffling noise. Lisa was a town girl at heart, but Rose was keen to share all the experiences of her new home with her friend and wanted her to embrace everything.

Lisa was the only other person that Rose had talked to about her mystery man that she had spotted from the house. This meant that Lisa was constantly on the lookout for him as she walked and reckoned that the faint snuffling noises that she had heard were him sleeping under the hedge waiting for her. Rose was very perturbed by her friend's train of thought and the thought of a strange man waiting for her under a hedge, however handsome, was very disturbing.

Lisa hugged Rose hard when she first saw the house.

"What a delight. You are so lucky," she remarked as they walked towards the front door. She laughed at the pots filled with the daffodils standing like sentries either side of the front door.

"Oh, you are silly, Rose my dear, flower filled pots at the door with a tumble-down house all around it."

Rose shared the joke, but explained, "The house is mine and I wanted to add something of myself to it." Lisa agreed with this sentiment, but they both thought that the recent bits that Lisa had brought with her should be kept somewhere safe while all the building work was going on.

The armchair that Rose had moved into the living room made the room look cosy, even though it was the only piece of furniture in the room. Although it still looked as if it had just been vacated even though Rose had pumped up the cushions on her last visit. The Captain's hat was still on the window seat overlooking the river and Lisa grabbed it and turned it repeatedly in her hands. Lisa had gone very quiet.

She stood at the window and stared across the river and the field beyond and said with a whisper, "I can hear the sea, the waves crashing on the shingle shore. I can smell the salty water from the sea."

Rose took the Captain's hat from her hands and replied, "I don't remember telling you that the beach was shingle. How do you know that?"

Lisa shook her head and shrugged her shoulders. "I just do, when I had that hat in my hands, I just knew all about the sea, the ocean, the beach …"

Lisa sat down on the window seat and drew her legs up under her. She rested her chin on her knees and continued to look out at the horizon. This was not how Rose imagined Lisa would have reacted to the house. She thought she would have run around the house like an excited toddler at a playground. Running from room to room and exhorting her vision for the place as if it were hers. There she was gazing dreamily out of the window, curled up and looking for all the world as if she were waiting for someone.

Rose dragged her from the window seat with a yell. She led her friend out to the kitchen and stood back and waited for her reaction. This time it was as she expected.

"This is not a kitchen, sweetie. This is a walk-in larder."

She unlocked the door and frowned as she looked out into the garden across to the building a little way away.

"No way, this is the back door? I was expecting it to open up to a farmhouse kitchen with big table in the middle and an Aga!"

Rose was relieved that the quiet, dreamy Lisa had gone. Her friend was back on sparkling form. She explained her ideas about putting some of the kitchen stuff in the outbuildings so not to spoil the fabric of the place. Rose could not believe it when Lisa agreed and did not push for a grand extension and a 'Country Living' type kitchen. It seemed that the Captain's House was working its magic on yet another person.

Lisa could not believe that the house had been empty since Great Aunt Lily Anne had died and that no one had come forward to claim it. She did not find the house creepy or scary and did not understand how the locals claimed it was. She thought that any empty house looked sad and unloved, and anything could look creepy in the dark. But Lisa was a girl who slept with the landing light on and knew exactly where the torch and candles were if there was a power cut. Her confidence and delight in an empty house over a certain age was out of character.

They looked around upstairs and Lisa took one look at the lumpy, smelly mattress and said, "You are not keeping that. There needs to be health warning on it."

"I was hoping that you would give me a hand to take it down the stairs," Rose said.

Lisa shook her head from side to side and slid into the next room to stop Rose offering her a corner of the mattress straight away. It was very unfortunate that she had slid into the bathroom. The smelliest and most uninviting room of the house. Lisa bid a hasty retreat and dashed into the back bedroom, with the telescope still parked in the middle of the floor. Her fingers caressed the worn brass and she once again gazed out of the window.

"Hey, look Rose, there is a man walking outside. He is rather nice. I saw this one first."

Rose followed her friend's gaze and to her surprise it was her handsome stranger.

"Oh no, my girl, that is my mystery man. Hands off, I saw him first."

This time the man did not look across at the house, he seemed to be in a hurry and they both watched as he marched off into the distance.

There was a clatter from downstairs. Lisa was sure the noise had come from the direction of the kitchen and dashed there, but Rose knew just where and what the noise was. She was right, the Captain's hat was once again on the floor, having fallen off the window seat. As she relayed all the other instances the Captain's hat had fallen to the floor in the house, Lisa's face lit up.

"My, you have a house with a resident ghost as well. Perhaps the Captain is trying to tell you something."

"Was that guy outside real or was he another ghost? No one else has seen him, but you and I, you know."

Twenty-Three

Back at the annexe, after a full day exploring the Captain's House and garden, the girls sat together looking at the plans of the property. Lisa was full of ideas, some good and some awful. She was sharing them all with Rose. Rose's head was spinning with all the ideas and she switched the television on, to distract her friend and give herself time to think. Glancing across at the clock and noticing the time she went to get ready for dinner at The Ship.

Rose chose her outfit with care, just in case she bumped into her mystery man in the pub and fussed with her hair and makeup. Lisa, although intrigued by her friend's behaviour, joined in the fun. It was a while since they had had a night out together. They were both looking forward to it. Rose told Lisa everything she knew about the pub's proprietors, Bob and Doreen.

The pub was not as busy as it was when she had gone out for dinner with Steve as the band were not playing. A few couples and some families were enjoying a meal together and a few of the locals were playing darts or sitting at the bar. There was no sign of Mickey and his dog Bert at the bar. Doreen was very attentive but did not want to chat. The meal was delivered promptly by a young waitress and Doreen watched over them from the bar. The meal itself was delicious. They both ate three courses and shared a bottle of wine. They talked about the Captain's House and the rather attractive stranger that could only be spied from the house. They kept an eye out for him all evening. Rose was certain he was real. Lisa was only teasing that he was ghostly figure. They could not be sure. However, they both felt that Doreen was keeping an eye on them!

Rose did not see the old pub sign anywhere and wanted to ask Doreen where it was, as she had previously said she was going to display it in the pub for everyone to see. Perhaps Bob and Doreen had second thoughts about that, maybe it was valuable. She was not going to ask to see it again, and as Mickey was not at the bar, there was no point anyway.

She pointed out the painting of the Captain's garden to Lisa at the table, but implored Lisa not to get up for a closer look. Lisa could see the lady standing in the flowers from her seat.

"You know it is not a traditional cottage garden. There are far too many roses. Big, old-fashioned roses that seem too heavy for their stems."

They were mainly pink and white and in full bloom. It was clear that it was painted in the height of the summer.

"The painting is enchanting. Do you think it is worth anything? The rumours suggest that it was painted by the Captain himself," Rose said.

"Oh, I don't think so, the style suggests a good century or two earlier, but I can't really see without a closer look. I would need to take it out of the frame and examine it," Lisa replied.

Lisa's mum and dad were antique art dealers and respected experts in their field. Lisa studied fine art at university and made a living as an artist. Lisa restored old paintings as hobby.

"Please let me get up for a closer look, Rose?" she pleaded and kicked her friend firmly but gently under the table.

"Perhaps there were more than one captain. Maybe there were generations of captains that all lived in the house?" Rose suggested.

Lisa was perplexed by this assumption as captains were generally wealthy and the Captain's House was rather small for a captain. Lisa's imagination was running wild now.

"I bet he was a wealthy landowner who fell in love with a woman of lowly status, and he was thrown out penniless, but he still married the woman he loved and lived in a rather lovely house near to the sea."

Rose laughed loudly and raised her eyes to the heavens. She adored her friend and loved the fact that she could be lost in the middle of a daydream at the slightest prompt. She knew that she had to bring her back down to earth with a bump so she suggested, "We better go up to the bar to pay our bar and dinner bill."

Money was guaranteed to bring her friend to her senses, as money seemed to slip through Lisa's fingers due to her shopping habits and generosity. However, when they got to the bar, Doreen was nowhere to be seen and she handed her credit card to the waitress that had served them at the table. Very strange they agreed on the drive back to the annexe, Rose wondered where she got to.

"She had her eyes on us all night," Rose said. "I felt her watching me and trying to catch what we were saying."

They both shivered and agreed that this was slightly worrying.

"Perhaps she has designs on your house?" Lisa wondered aloud.

Rose was woken during the night by a clatter, just like the Captain's hat falling again she mused, still half asleep. She sat up and looked around at the bedroom in the annexe. She felt anxious about her Captain's House, empty and dark along the lane. Why would she dream about his hat? It only fell down if someone was in the house. She wanted to leap out of bed to check on the property but knew there was nothing in there worth stealing and she had checked every nook and cranny in the place.

She just hoped it was a dream and that she would not find anything amiss when she went there in the morning. Rose then knew that she had to move into the Captain's House as soon as she could. She would be happy for the work to go on around her and she was confident that Steve would respect her privacy. It would be nice seeing her house being put back together, being right there in the thick of it. It made sense making sure it was done right. She would give Steve a ring in the morning.

The house emitted a warm, welcoming glow in the surrounding darkness. It appeared clean and the chimney was straight and true. The paintwork was freshly painted, the flowers bloomed in the garden. Tonight the shadows were in the garden, working together side by side tending the flowers and vegetables. A cat scampered around the garden. The waiting was over, or so it seemed.

Twenty-Four

Rose was rudely awakened by Lisa bouncing on her bed, imploring her to get up and get back to their Captain's House. Rose was amazed that Lisa was up once again at an unearthly hour. It must be the magic of the house. It seemed to galvanise people and motivate them into putting it right. However, this philosophy was at complete odds with the fact that the house had stood empty for a while.

Rose was feeling quite seasick at Lisa's continual bouncing. She tempted Lisa with the promise of a cooked breakfast and padded into the kitchen to cook it for her. Lisa followed, grinning insanely and talking ten to the dozen about all the things that could be done to their Captain's House.

"You have said 'our' Captain's House since you have got up. Something you want to share?" said Rose to her friend as she was frying the bacon.

Lisa sighed dramatically and replied, "OK, your house is special. I cannot explain it, but I feel connected to the place and it just pops out, when I say 'ours'. You and I have been friends for so long, just feels so right. After all, what is yours is mine and what is mine is mine, don't you think?"

Rose was reminded of a trinket that Lisa had bought her for Christmas when they were teenagers. It was a pot to keep loose change in, and it was Lisa's attempt to keep her tidy and stop her throwing her money on the side and losing it. It was inscribed with the very same phrase, 'What is yours is mine and what is mine is mine'.

Rose was secretly pleased that Lisa was as fond of the house as she was, and it was comforting to know that if she was ever feeling despondent about the house, she would be able to call on her friend, who would be on her side. When they had finished their breakfast, Rose mentioned hearing a clatter during the night and her fears about the Captain's House being empty. So, instead of just wandering back to the house and thinking about the latter stages of the renovations, they decided to visit the property with a view to seeing if she could live there while the renovations were going on around her. They discussed the basic requirements that she would need to live there. Although there was electricity and power, she needed Steve to ensure that it was safe, and she needed to run the tap and check the water quality.

When they arrived at the house, they both made their way to the bench, which always toppled over during the night. This time it was lying on its back with its legs in the air. When they righted the bench and sat down, the obvious problems with the chimney stack glared at them from where they were sitting as they looked back at the house. It looked very unsafe, and Rose knew that Steve would not let her move in until he was sure that the property was liveable.

"Another person looking out for me," Rose mused out loud.

Lisa said, "Yeah, but he is being paid to do so. He is your builder, isn't he?"

The sound of crunching gravel made both girls jump, and they turned to see who was driving into the driveway. Steve tooted the horn on his Triumph Herald in greeting and Lisa raised her eyebrows at Rose. "Oh, I think I could live here, if this is the quality of the visitors!" Lisa said. Steve was passing by and saw someone in the garden and wanted to check that the visitors were genuine, as he could only see the tops of their heads from the road.

"You are supposed to be looking where you are going when you are driving," Rose scolded.

After introducing Lisa to Steve, Rose outlined the reason for her visit and waited for Steve to answer. She picked up a blade of long grass and ran it through her fingers as she waited. Steve seemed to take ages to answer. Finally, he explained gently that it would be another couple of weeks at least, as work was needed on the chimney and he wanted to check all the amenities for her before she moved in. Seeing her face, he grabbed her hand and pulled her closer to him.

"You would be more comfortable at Little Lanterns, until the weather changes, as the nights are still cold," he said, with a sexy wink at Rose, "but why don't you spend most of the day at the house while we are working next week, and you can make your mind up then?"

Lisa smiled sweetly at Steve and whispered behind her hand at Rose, "You would have to spend more time with him then. Don't forget his nights are so cold, too."

Steve explained that she would need power, water, but no heating if it was the summer and there was no way that anyone could sweep the chimney, so she couldn't have a fire until it was repaired and at least standing straight and upright. They all traipsed around the house together and came across the mattress on the floor in the entrance to the main bedroom. Steve picked up a corner of it. "You will need a sleeping bag for a while." Rose looked at the old brass bed frame and thought of how it was when she first came to the house, with the bed made with the rose eiderdown on top.

"I think I will just get a new mattress and make up a proper bed when the time comes. I will be heaps more comfortable."

Muttering about the complexities of women, Steve made his way down the stairs. Lisa and Rose giggled together as they heard him say, "The house is a wreck, but she wants a proper bed all done up, wonders will never cease."

The kitchen was their next stop and they stood in the doorway and surveyed the small space. Rose entered the room and stood squarely in the middle with her arms crossed.

"This kitchen is perfect and is just right for my Captain's House. I agree it needs an oven, and maybe a tiny fridge, but all the other white goods will have to go in one of the buildings over there," she said as she swept her arm over towards the back door.

"I was thinking we could rip it all out and replace it with a modern kitchen with a trendy black theme," Steve retorted with gales of laughter, raising his hands in front of his face ready for the blows. Rose gasped and then saw he was joking and joined in.

Rose had her serious face on when she stopped laughing and stated firmly, "I love the kitchen as it is and don't want to change it as it would spoil the whole feel of the house."

Twenty-Five

The next few weeks passed in a blur for Rose. She did not have time to miss her friend's company. She popped next door into Val's if she needed some female company once or twice a week. She had plenty of male company during the daytime at the Captain's House. Val always had something on the go for dinner that she could stretch to three and she always made Rose feel very welcome. Rose was very cosy at 'Little Lanterns but was very conscious of the changing seasons and knew the summer months were very clearly on their way by a sharp rise in temperature and an increase in daylight hours, it was time for Rose to seriously consider moving into the Captain's House.

Steve and his builder colleagues had been busy with the house and Rose had been taking refreshments to the lads in the afternoons for several weeks now. Flasks of tea and coffee that were always piping hot as it was only a short walk from Little Lanterns to the Captain's House. Rose was fond of cakes and biscuits and kept a constant supply for her and the boys. She pottered about while the work was going on. Just wandering, thinking, and enjoying the thrill of the anticipation – a finished house and then finally a home.

Steve was brilliant coordinating the work for her and making sure that the project was running to time. He was fair with everyone and the work was proving to be excellent. The chimney stack was now standing upright and tall and that made the house feel different. The hustle and bustle of the builders and suppliers coming and going made the house feel alive again and not lonely and forlorn as it once was.

Every time Rose went into the village for her daily newspaper, people would stop her and ask her how things were progressing with the house. The footpath on the other side of the river was becoming busier as the locals found excuses to walk that way and have a crafty nose at the work in progress.

Rose was worried that all the goings on would change the feel of the place, but once everyone had gone home for the day, the house seemed to revert to its natural state and was hers and her Captain's once again. The afternoon sunlight and the ever-lengthening days meant that Rose could linger in the property until dusk fell most days. As dusk drew in, she sat in the armchair looking across at the river towards the sea and daydreamed about the house and pondered on the Captain. She often picked up the Captain's hat and fondled it in her hands as she dreamed. It was kept on the window seat and had stopped falling to the floor whenever she was in the property. Rose was sure that this was because the Captain approved of the work and had no need to make his feelings known.

However, this was to change the next time Rose found herself dozing in her favourite armchair in the late afternoon sunshine. She was curled up with her legs underneath her and was holding an OS map of the area that Steve had dug out for her. Earlier, she had been looking at the view and the map and could see why the house was built in this position. The river, the footpath, and the proximity to the sea made it an ideal property for a seaman. The clatter as the hat tumbled to the floor downstairs woke her long before the intruder entered the property and she jumped to her feet and hid behind the open door of the bedroom. At first, she thought it was Steve, but he always called out before he entered the property and she had given him a key. The back door was being rattled on its hinges and shoved open. Rose shivered and squeezed further into the tiny triangular space. She could hear heavy boots on the floorboards and then tramping up the stairs. The footsteps continued to resonate through the house as the intruder paced about.

Rose snatched up the map and fled downstairs and out through the open back door into the garden, across the lane and raced back to Little Lanterns. David was in the garden and, when he saw how distressed she was, rushed to meet Rose on the driveway. On the way back to the house, Rose worried that the intruder might be violent and perhaps they should have called the police. David took Rose's arm gently and turned her to face him at the roadside.

"Listen, if it sounds like they are still in property or there is a strange car outside we will call the police from the lane."

Rose agreed with this plan of action and in a few moments they were standing side by side looking over the hedge into the garden of the Captain's House. The front door was wide open, but there was no sign of anyone.

"Oh no, I went out the back door and that was the door that was wrenched open. I did not leave the front door open," Rose exclaimed in a whisper.

They waited for a few minutes to see if anyone came in or out and then agreed to enter the house. Together they checked the house, room by room, and did not find any evidence of an intruder. Retracing their steps to the kitchen, Rose took a good look around. The back door was open as well, but it was not damaged nor broken. David queried whether she had locked the door when she was in the property, but Rose could not remember. As she gazed at the floor, she noticed a slight trail of sand that seemed to trace a line out into the hallway. She followed it and noticed that it went up the stairs and into each room. Rose found herself cuddling the Captain's hat for comfort as she discussed with David what she should do next. She agreed to return to Little Lanterns for a cup of tea and maybe dinner with him and Val.

Before Rose left the house, she carefully replaced the Captain's hat on the window seat.

The house and garden were invisible in the darkness that evening. Not a glimpse could be seen of the house from the lane. No lights or warm glows were visible through the glass. It was as if the house was no more. The garden could not have been more of a contrast. The vegetation was at least an average man's head height and was so tightly wound together that an insect would have had trouble trying to move about amongst the leaves. The house was safe and secure within its living fortress. It would not be breached again.

Twenty-Six

The following day, Rose popped over to the Captain's House first thing and took her morning cuppa with her in her flask, together with a couple of extra flasks for any additional builders that would be there first thing. She wanted to speak to Steve and ask him if he could remember locking the back and front door when he left the house yesterday afternoon. She was worried about the events of the day before and was unable to eat any breakfast until she had spoken with Steve. She could have texted or rang him the night before, but she was too rattled and did not want to sound like a feeble woman. David and Val had fussed over her all evening and it was late before she was able to make her excuses and head off to bed. She had fallen asleep straight away but was not refreshed by her night's slumber.

Steve was just getting out of his van when she approached the side garden, and he took one look at her worried face and hurried to her side.

"What is wrong, Rose?" he asked her. Rose explained yesterday's events and asked him the all-important questions about what he did when he left the property the day before. Steve shook his head and looked down at the floor, kicking the dust with his feet.

"I would not have locked you in the house," he replied, "but the front door was definitely locked as we came through the back all day."

Steve unlocked the front door and they both stared at the line of sand that made its way up the stairs. It could not be missed as the floorboards were dark and grimy and the sand was bright against the dark wood. Rose leaned against Steve for support and Steve wound his arm around her and held her tight.

"It might be some kid's idea of a joke or perhaps that scruffy guy was trying to scare you off," Steve suggested. "I will ask around when we go to the pub this evening as well, someone must know where he is hanging around. If he is scaring you, then I will have to have words with him," he said with a snarl.

Rose was sure it could not have been Christian. He had kept away from the house and had not been seen in the village for some time. Although she was keen to look at the stuff in the outbuildings, she did not want to disturb his things, so she had left everything as it was. One of the buildings was empty when she had first arrived. It was in this building that Steve fitted a new lock and kept his building supplies in.

They were interrupted in their deliberations by George and James appearing at the front door. Steve explained what had happened the day before and asked them both to be extra vigilant during the day, especially if they were working in a room overlooking the footpath, to see if anyone was showing an unusual amount of interest in the house.

"That scruffy guy will rue the day he ever messed with Rose and this house, if it does turn out to be him. We will sort him out, what do you think, fellas?" Steve was cross, and this was the first time that Rose had seen him with his hackles up. She was alarmed by the turn of the conversation.

"Don't be so ridiculous, we don't even know it was him yet. You are making assumptions. If anyone knows where he is, just let me know. I am sure he is a good guy really."

George and James went off to the outbuilding to get their tools and Steve and Rose were left alone again.

Rose was bemused to discover that Steve still had his arm draped around her shoulder and she shrugged it off and made her way up the stairs. Steve followed close behind when he saw that she was following the trail of sand. The sand went in all the rooms, but there was a lot of sand in the landing at the top of the stairs, in a nice tidy pile. Very bizarre! They both looked up at the loft hatch as the pile of sand was right underneath it. Steve went and retrieved his ladder from the bedroom and opened the hatch, propped up the ladder, and disappeared into the darkness. Taking a torch from his trouser pocket he shone it around in the loft space.

After a short while, he made his way down the ladder and stood in front of Rose.

"I need to get the lads to come up there with me. It is just as I left it, but I have seen something wedged under the eaves that I have not noticed before. It could be wadding, to stop the draught or wet getting in. It could just be a bird's nest, but I think I should check it out."

Steve was very thorough, and Rose was a little worried that he had not noticed this before. However, she was reassured that she did not hear the loft hatch open while she was in the property yesterday and there was no sign of any trail of sand in the loft space.

Steve, James, and George joined Rose on the landing, all of them holding torches. Steve glanced across at Rose and handed her a torch.

"Looking at your face, I can assume that you want to join us up there," he said with a smile.

"You bet," replied Rose, "I was sure that I was going to miss out on the excitement, because you all look rather excited about something."

They all traipsed up the ladder and huddled together in the bigger part of the loft space. Steve crouched down and edged his way towards the strange package under the eaves. With four torches on it, it was clear that it was not a bird's nest as it was far too large and a funny shape. Rose held her breath. The shape resembled a dead body.

Twenty-Seven

Steve crouched as far as he could into the space, right underneath the eaves, but could not reach the object with his outstretched arm. He lay down and edged his way towards it, shuffling along on his stomach. As his hand made contact with the packaging, it made a rustling noise and made everyone jump. It appeared to be tarpaulin or something similar covering the object. Steve pulled a corner of the covering but could not dislodge it. It was stuck fast into the eaves and roofing timbers. George and James joined Steve on their bellies and they all took a section of the covering and like a large three-headed insect they tugged and pulled the cover in unison.

A loud scrapping noise and an ominous creak signified that it was coming loose and with a massive tug they dislodged it from its hiding place. It was heavy, and the men had trouble moving it towards the middle of the loft space. They all scrambled to their feet, as they were now standing in the largest part of the loft space, looking down at the large bundle of tarred canvas in front of them. Their torches were all pointing at the object which looked very sinister.

Rose shivered and requested that they uncover whatever it was downstairs in one of the bedrooms. No one disagreed. They manhandled the object down through the loft hatch and into the back room with the telescope. Once again, they all stood in a circle and stared. No one wanted to touch it.

"It felt like a body and was heavy like a body," remarked James as he retreated towards the door. George followed him. Then it was just Rose and Steve staring. Rose knelt down and looked closely at the package. The tarred canvas was tied tightly with rope and Rose was trying to find the all-important knot to unravel the curious object. Steve rolled the item on its side to reveal a knot and they both worked together to untie the rope. All at once, the job was done. The canvas was loose around the thing. Rose was becoming impatient and suddenly did not care if it was a dead body or the Captain's long-lost treasure, she just wanted to find out what it was.

The canvas fell away at one end and two bright eyes looked out from the package. Rose gasped and grabbed Steve's arm. Steve took the other end of the canvas and unraveled the whole object and what was inside took their breath away.

"It's a body, but not a dead one," Steve stated and knelt for a closer look. Rose knelt beside him and took another look for herself.

"Oh, she is so beautiful," she said, "what was she doing in the loft and what do we do with her now?"

Struggling to comprehend what was in front of them, Steve and Rose tried to stand her up. Their efforts proved unsuccessful, and, in the end, they propped her up against the curve of the bay window. She was looking inwards towards the centre of the room but looked as though she belonged. Of course, she would belong. This was the Captain's House, and she was the most amazing figurehead that both Steve and Rose had ever seen. She seemed to be in almost perfect condition and her paint was still fairly bright. She had a whiff of the ocean about her. The base of the body where she would have been fixed to the bow of the ship was worn away. Her petticoats and dress were missing some paint. This did not detract from the peaceful and serene expression that was on the woman's face and her bright, inquisitive eyes that seemed to be full of knowing. Her lips were slightly smiling and plump. Her pretty dress revealed her ample bosom, and her delicate hands held a bunch of red and white roses.

Rose was so taken aback by what they had found that she had forgotten that George and James were still in the house. George was calling up the stairs, asking whether it was safe to come back upstairs and if they had to call the police. This was the second time within 24 hours that someone had asked Rose if they should call the police. Steve called both of them to come upstairs and not to be such cowards.

George and James entered the room and both looked at the figurehead, stunned. Expecting a dead body and then being confronted by a wooden lady smiling sweetly holding some flowers, it knocked them both for six. They all caught each other's eyes and started to giggle and then laugh at their earlier antics.

"It did look like a dead body wrapped up in that canvas, like a shroud," James stuttered, as he laughed.

The front door gave a bang and before they could all get worried, Rose heard her dad shouting up the stairs.

"Thought I would pop over to see how you are doing and it sounds like you are having a party, can anyone join in?" Rose greeted her dad with a smile and winked at him from the top of the stairs.

"You better come up and meet this lovely lady in the back bedroom. She must have some connection to my Captain."

Twenty-Eight

Her dad entered the room and joined the rest of them standing in a semi-circle around the figurehead. "I thought you meant a real lady, not a wooden one. She is a rather fine specimen is she not!" he exclaimed, returning Rose's wink with a knowing smile. Rose gently herded all the men away from the figurehead and back downstairs and busied herself in the kitchen with the flasks of hot water, making everyone a hot drink of their choice.

Her dad wandered off on his own and explored the house and ran his fatherly eyes over the work that had already taken place. The bathroom still retained a peculiar aroma as no one had been able to work out what was causing the smell. The roof was now watertight, and the dampness had been eradicated. He wandered out into the garden and sat on the bench and gazed at the house. Rose sat down beside him and followed his gaze. He was looking at the chimney, looking straight and standing tall. When his gaze returned to Rose, he nodded his head in approval.

"The house is safe now and watertight. Although, it appears to have another mistress in that upstairs bedroom!"

Rose thought her dad would be the best person to advise if the house was ready to live in and asked the all-important question.

"Do you think I could live here, while the rest of the work is going on, Dad?"

Her dad agreed with her and reckoned that she could move in, but she would have to live on takeaways as the oven was not ready to go yet. Rose's dad was ever practical and full of sensible advice, although she did not always take his advice. She agreed to wait until she had all the basic amenities ready to go. James overheard this part of the conversation and interrupted, "I am going as fast as I can with the electrics but want everything safe for you. You should not have to wait much longer. Why not order the oven and fridge that you want, and we could put them in the outhouse with our tools if they arrive too early? When I am ready, they will be all here and then we will just have to move them to their final spots in the kitchen."

Pete, Rose's dad, stayed at the house with Rose for the rest of the day. He helped with some of the easy jobs with Steve, James, and George. They enjoyed having an extra willing pair of hands that did their bidding with no questions asked. Rose popped back to the annexe and made a picnic for them all at lunchtime. The day went past in a flash.

Rose, however, was drawn to the figurehead and wasted lots of time just looking at her. She examined her carefully and found a series of strange carvings at her rear, very similar to those she had found on the back of the window seat. She took her phone out and took several photographs of the figurehead and some close ups of the carvings. She had to conclude that she was extremely well made and almost life-like. Rose had to stop herself from having a conversation with her. She felt that if she asked her questions, she would become an animate object and might just answer her!

The light started to fade, and the guys started to pack their things. Her dad came looking for her.

"The guys told me what happened here yesterday with the intruder. Perhaps you should all leave at the same time, or you should make a conscious effort to lock the doors behind them when they leave." Rose agreed with her dad but wondered if she should ask Steve to put the figurehead in his van and transport it to Little Lanterns for safekeeping. Steve had already pre-empted that question and was wrapping her back into the canvas that she was found in when Rose made her mind up. They all manhandled her once again down the stairs and placed her very carefully into the back of Steve's van.

A few minutes later, they all arrived back at Little Lanterns. Rose could not resist knocking on Val's door to see if she were in and to show her what they had found. Val was in, as she was busy getting ready for some guests that were due to arrive any minute, but she left her hoovering and followed Steve and Pete into the Little Lanterns with their intriguing package. She also remarked that it looked like a dead body and wanted whatever it was put away out of sight in case her new guest arrived early.

"Can you imagine what a scandal that would be around the village, a dead body at the local B &B. Oh goodness!" she exclaimed with a wry grin.

The men laid the canvas wrapped parcel down on the floor and then unwrapped her with great care then with a flourish stood the contents upright, leaning her against the window frame for extra support. Val was incredulous at the sight of the figurehead and was speechless for several minutes.

David had found the hoover in the doorway and his front door was wide open. He could see Steve's van in his drive with the rear doors also open. He went to look for his wife and he joined them at this very moment to see what all the commotion was about. He stared in disbelief at his wife's silence and the figurehead standing before him.

"Did she come from your Captain's house?" David asked. "She looks very familiar ... but where have I seen her before?"

Twenty-Nine

Rose enjoyed the unexpected catch up with her dad, but the events of the day had unnerved her. It was only a flying visit from her dad. He had left shortly after David's shocking announcement that he recognised the figurehead from somewhere. Steve had lingered on for the evening, Rose was grateful for the company and Steve was only too happy to provide it. They had ended up scoffing curry from the freezer and sharing a bottle of wine.

Their relationship was developing into a deep friendship and Rose really valued his opinion. She admitted to Steve that the Captain's House seemed to be taking over her life, she even confided in him that she was not sure about the figurehead being in the annexe with her during the night.

"You are not scared of a piece of wood, are you? It is just a girl," Steve teased. Rose was very indignant about the 'just a girl' comment and retaliated by swiping him with one of the sofa cushions. Steve gently nudged her with another cushion, which resulted in a full-scale cushion fight. All of a sudden, Rose found herself pinned down to the sofa with Steve's face just inches from her own. She was so tempted to reach up and kiss him but turned away just that little bit too fast and promptly fell in an ungainly heap at the side of the sofa. The thud and vibration caused the figurehead to rock and Steve leapt up and caught it in his arms before she toppled over.

"This is not the girl that I wanted in my arms" he joked, looking back at Rose on the floor.

"Oh, I am fine, thank you," said Rose, getting up onto her feet.

They both stood once again looking at the figurehead and Steve said, "You know I am happy to take her back to my house for the night if you really do not want her to stay." He then looked at Rose and with a sexy grin that went from ear to ear and back again, he said, "Or I could take this fine figure of a woman," wrapping an arm around Rose's waist, "you could come back to mine and keep me company!"

Rose was tempted to joke that he invited the figurehead first before her but was not sure how he would react. She was now very sure that Steve would have kissed her back, if she had tempted him, just a moment ago on the sofa.

There was an awkward silence for a moment.

Rose then knew that it was her job to keep the figurehead safe. Surely the figurehead could not do her any harm, as Rose was sure that she belonged to the Captain.

"Perhaps we should just wedge her into a more secure position and let her look out of the window, instead of at me."

Together they manoeuvred her into a stable position and Rose noticed that the base was very uneven as if it had been part of the original ship. They did not return to the sofa, and Steve left shortly after helping Rose place the figurehead somewhere secure, so she could not fall over during the night.

Rose had enjoyed the evening and was really looking forward to making the Captain's House her home, so that she could invite her friends around for the weekend and for dinner. Most of her friends were back in town, so she was more likely to have to have them stay for weekends and holidays. She did not feel too despondent, as she had made new friends in the village in the short time she had been staying there and would not be short of company in the meantime. She made a mental note to ask Steve over to the Captain's House when she had officially moved in and hoped he would be one of her first dinner guests.

Rose was happier with the figurehead now she was facing looking out of the window as she had felt that she was looking at her, watching her every move. She tidied up the dinner plates and stacked them next to the sink for washing up in the morning as she was feeling very tired. She took herself to bed and fell into a deep sleep as soon as her head hit the pillow.

She dreamt of the sea and a large ship with lots of sails, flapping in the wind. The noise of the sea, sails, and men shouting was very loud. She could feel the motion of the ship on the waves and was lulled into a deeper sleep by the rocking motion. The wind grew in intensity. She was swept into the air with the sea birds, flying and swooping up and down with them. She looked down at the ship and found herself gliding towards the front of the ship, until she was looking straight into her figurehead's eyes. They glinted at her and her gaze was drawn to the full, painted lips which smiled, making her pert nose lift gently. She then opened her mouth and started to speak to Rose, but her speech was taken by the wind and Rose could not make out what she was saying. It seemed important. The lady then looked down at her hands and smiled at the roses she was holding and then directly up at a distant figure peering over the side of the boat and meeting her gaze. It was the captain himself that was holding the lady's gaze. Their Captain, Rose surmised, their Captain.

This dream was so vivid that Rose remembered every detail of it for days afterwards. She would puzzle over the detail in the quiet moments over the next few weeks when she was alone at the

Captain's House. She did not share the dream with anyone but kept puzzling and wondering what the figurehead was saying to her. The way the figurehead turned into a real lady in her dream and held the gaze of her Captain tantalized Rose and kept her guessing. Rose was not scared of the figurehead since the dream and hoped that the lady was once the mistress of her house.

Rose spent some time on the internet learning about figureheads and the type of ship they would be at the front of. She was intrigued by all the detail she had found. She was still searching for where David could have recognised her from, perhaps he had been mistaken.

Thirty

The weather had turned warmer and in turn the Captain's garden was now a jungle of greenery and unidentified flowers. The house could barely be seen from the roadside because of all the vegetation. The fruit trees had blossomed. The garden was unrecognisable from when she had first viewed the house. The house was slowly coming together and was cleaner and brighter than its gloomy, dusty state that she had seen on that first blustery, wet afternoon.

Rose had changed as well. Not having to go into an office and deal with somebody else's business, in comparison to dealing with something completely new but special to her every day, had changed her personality. She was more forward thinking and still careful with her money. Steve, George and James, were also being very careful with her money and were all keen to finish the house within budget. She was so lucky to have found them.

It was all becoming very real and living in her Captain's house was a certainty, not just a wishful dream. Rose had gone back to her rented property in London to get some more appropriate clothes for the summer months and she even packed her swimming costume and bikini in order to take advantage of the beach nearby. Her home in town did not seem right for her anymore and she packed her small car with as much stuff as she could possibly fit in. She would have to give notice and empty the place soon, so she could save on her rent.

She knew that she would have to return to the office at some stage as the money would not last forever. She would have to pay huge train fares travelling in from rural Kent and would waste a massive chunk of her day travelling.

Val was busy with lots of guests and did not have any vacancies for the near future. Rose was more than ready to move out of Little Lanterns. She was very appreciative of Val's warm-hearted gesture of letting her stay in the newly renovated annexe for a cut down rent, but as the pace of the Bed and Breakfast guests was picking up for the summer, Val needed Little Lanterns back. The Captain's House was ready for her to move in to, but work would still need to go on around her for a little longer. It was so typical of Val not to have asked Rose when the Captain's House would be ready. She had not even hinted. Val was a real sweetheart and Rose felt very privileged to count her as a friend.

Little Lantern's seemed to be full to the brim with all of Rose's belongings and when Steve came to pick her up en route to the house, he could hardly fit inside the door. Over coffee that very afternoon at the Captain's House, the guys decided that they would move Rose in the following day. Steve, George, and James all had trade vans, so it would not be a problem to move all her stuff from the annexe to the house. Steve had added some extra locks to the front and back doors and had even added a chain to the front door for even more security. When Rose mentioned that she still had a rented property in London, all the guys offered to help her clear that and ferry her additional bits down to the Kent coast in their vans as well. Her new oven and fridge were now fitted into the kitchen, the taps when turned on were gushing clear, clean water and the boiler was heating the hot water to a pleasing temperature.

For all her impatience to move in, Rose had procrastinated in the last couple of weeks and made excuse after excuse. The guys could see this and were keen to stop her pointless excuses and help her achieve her dream of moving in once and for all into her Captain's House.

Rose was so excited and tried not to show it to Steve and the others, but it was clear to see. They all traipsed off to the pub to celebrate as it was clear that no one was going to get anything done with all the chatter and waves of excitement that were emanating from Rose. They packed up and with a quick phone call to Val and David to invite them to the impromptu gathering they made their way to The Ship. It was early afternoon, but the pub was busy in the early summer sunshine and they found a table next to the window by sheer luck. It was a tight squeeze when Val and David arrived, but that just added to the fun. Val ordered a bottle of champagne at the bar and they all toasted the Captain's House.

Bob and Doreen had come out from behind the bar and joined in the celebration, bringing over some food for them all to nibble on. However, Rose was still uncertain of Doreen's intentions towards her and the Captain's House and was very wary of Doreen. Doreen, however, was in her element, being the perfect hostess and announcing that the food was on the house. She was full of questions about the Captain's House and what they had found. Everyone had agreed to keep the discovery of the figurehead in the attic to themselves for the time being, but as the afternoon wore on, it was proving more difficult.

David was the quieter one of the couples. He was sitting to the edge of the gathering. All of a sudden, he injected in an uncharacteristically loud voice, "That's where I have seen her face before, right there."

Thirty-One

This was greeted with a stunned silence and everyone looked at David first and then at Rose. Rose found that her curiosity overcame her need for secrecy, and she completely forgot that Doreen and Bob had joined them at their table. David had got to his feet and was examining the painting of the Captain's garden. He peered closely at the canvas, which made Val giggle and raise her glass to her husband. "Ahem, do you need glasses, my dear? Or are you getting old?" Val, even though she was one of the last to arrive, had consumed more than her share of the champagne.

Rose got up and stood beside David and peered at the same spot in the painting. "Oh my god," she exclaimed with a sharp intake of breath, "that's how you recognised her, she is the lady in the garden. Look everyone, come and see." As everyone crowded round to look at the lady in the garden, Doreen and Bob were left at the table looking very bemused and rather worried.

"So, she was real, and my dad was right – she was the true mistress of the house. How exciting," Rose chattered to everyone. "This is supposed to be painted by my Captain, so it figures."

David was very relieved, "I thought that I was going mad when I said that I recognised her, where on earth would I have met someone wearing that get up? How on earth would I have passed up a date with that pretty lady?"

Val snorted into her drink, retorting, "Chance would be a fine thing. At least the competition is definitely dead."

Doreen and Bob looked even more puzzled at this turn in conversation and despite her reservations and previous warnings from Val, Rose decided to let them in on their discovery. She was in the middle of explaining their recent find at the Captain's House when she caught a glimpse of Steve's face and saw his eyes flashing a warning. It was already too late, and Doreen and Bob were enthusing about the figurehead and speculating about its worth.

Rose and everyone else had not considered the fact that the figurehead could be worth lots of money. Everyone until then had just reveled in her beauty and grace. The colours of the paint, which had faded but still retained some warmth. The quality of the carving and the delightful expression on her face. The beautiful roses that were contained in her delicate hands. The fact that she might be worth any money was a bonus that Rose genuinely had not considered. She was part of the Captain's House and Rose was extremely fond of her already. Rose had worked out that she would place her in the upstairs room with the Captain's telescope. The figurehead would then be able to gaze out at the sea in the far distance, where she once belonged with the Captain, as she had visualised in her unforgettable vivid dream.

Finding her amongst the flowers put an entirely different spin on things, but it explained the flowers in her hands. Trust Doreen and Bob to want to get a valuation on her, it just showed how different their viewpoint was to hers. She wondered if that was why they hid the pub sign from sight so quickly and wondered if she had misjudged them. They always seemed to want to know what was going on with the Captain's House. Steve had told her that they had pumped him for information on the house on more than one occasion. Did they know that the figurehead was hidden in the loft or was there something else hidden somewhere else that they wanted her to find? Was it them who had frightened her when she was on her own in the house and had left a trail of sand for her to find as a tantalising clue?

Looking more closely at Bob and Doreen's expressions, Rose scrutinised their faces as discreetly as she could. It looked like genuine surprise on both their faces, but Rose was not sure.

They all took their places around the table once again and David found himself the centre of attention. Glasses were raised once again to David and his 'other women'. A quiet, reserved man by nature, David was uncomfortable with all the attention and soon drew the conversation back to Rose moving into the Captain's House the following day. Plans were drawn up and jobs allocated, and Rose sat back and listened to her new friends sort her new house out. It seemed surreal, but very nice and Rose felt those strange little wobbles in the pit of her stomach that you get before a big day or Christmas morning.

There was a sudden surge of customers to the pub as the evening drew in and Doreen and Bob had to attend the bar. This prompted Val and David to leave to tend to their existing guests and welcome new ones that were arriving. George and James had plans for the evening and it was just Steve and Rose remaining. It reminded Rose of their evening out when she had first arrived and her one and only ride in his prized classic car. Steve had asked her out in the evening several times since but she had always turned him down, preferring to spend some time alone in the evening. She was normally trawling the internet for nautical knowledge or sourcing items for the house. Rose had great fun finding items for the kitchen and the utility outhouse in the yard. Finding the smaller specifications to fit such a small space in the kitchen and then letting rip in the large utility area with the larger, flashy units that she would have loved in a brand-new modern kitchen.

She had spent lots of time with Steve, but only in the Captain's House and her lodgings, not on another formal date. She enjoyed his company but had not forgotten her mystery man she had spotted. Rose was glad that Lisa had seen the mystery man as well, or she would have thought she had imagined him. Rose was debating in her head whether to eat dinner with Steve in the pub tonight or to make her excuses once again and ask for a lift back to the annexe to sort her stuff out ready for the morning and moving day.

Thirty-Two

Rose eventually asked Steve to give her a lift back to the annexe that night as she could not settle at the pub for dinner. She had too much to do. She spent the evening sorting out the annexe and making sure that everything was ready to go in the morning.

Now that the morning was here, Rose was beside herself with anticipation and worry. Her nerves were getting the better of her. She was pacing up and down alongside the window, waiting for anyone to arrive long before they were due. Eventually, she stood next to the figurehead and was unintentionally mirroring her position when Steve drew into the driveway in his van.

Steve turned the engine off and just sat staring at the two of them in the window, the resemblance was uncanny. Rose and the figurehead had the same wistful expression in their eyes and face and the only thing that was missing was the flowers in Rose's hands. However, she did not need the flowers to complete the comparison as her name was Rose. Steve was transfixed and rooted to the driver's seat, lost in thought, so he jumped when Val appeared at the window, "Are you OK?" Val then followed his gaze and looked back at the window. "Goodness, that it is spooky," she whispered. "They look so alike and they are wearing the same expression and everything …"

Then Rose disappeared from the window and reappeared somber and wistful outside the window. It had just dawned on her that today was the day she had been looking forward to, ever since she had first seen the house and it was finally here. Val was the only one that seemed to have retained the excitement of the day before, and even she announced that she was putting the kettle on for coffee and cake before they got started. In next to no time, there was a coffee morning in full swing at Val's. George and James joined in when they arrived. They had even started on a Victoria Sponge that was intended for the afternoon when everything was finished.

It did not take long to move Rose's stuff into the Captain's House as she only had boxes, clothes, and shopping. She had rented a fully furnished flat and was staying in Val's fully furnished annexe, so she had no furniture to move. Nothing big and bulky, apart from the figurehead, which was returning home with Rose to the Captain's House once more.

Rose and Val spent the morning bossing the men about, making sure that the right boxes were placed in the right rooms. The fridge was filled with food, milk, and wine. The kettle was permanently on the boil and mugs were scattered across the wooden worktop. The Captain's House was no longer empty and quiet, but full of people, noise, and chatter. Each room had lots of boxes in it and the house was starting to feel like a home again, albeit a messy, cluttered one.

Rose had ordered a new mattress for the original bed and that had been delivered to the house several days before, so that just needed to be taken up to the bedroom to finish the move, with the old mattress taken outside to be dumped in its place in one of the outbuildings. As the men placed the mattress on the bed, Rose was watching, as it was the final job to be done. Rose gave a big sigh and flopped into the armchair opposite. She looked across at the box marked 'Bedding' in a black marker pen and decided that she would make the bed up when she was on her own.

There was nothing more for anyone to do and Rose sat quietly waiting for everyone to come to that same conclusion. They had all been such a help that Rose could not bring herself to chuck them out or invite them to leave, just because she was desperate to be on her own. Steve, James, and George padded down the stairs and she could hear them chatting to Val about what more needed to be done.

Realising that Rose had not followed them downstairs and was enjoying the peace upstairs in her new house they agreed unanimously that it was time to go and leave Rose to it. A chorus of 'goodbyes' sounded up the stairs and Rose finally had the house to herself. She heard Steve check the doors were locked before he left, first the front door and then the back. When he was satisfied that she was safe and secure, he looked up at the window to catch her eye. Then he was off too.

Rose took her trainers off and curled up in the chair, resting her head on the Captain's coat that was still hanging on the back of the chair where she had first found it. She felt cosy and warm and very, very happy. There was a long way to go to make the Captain's House a proper home. All the walls needed re-plastering and painting. The wood in some of the windows was rotten and needed replacing, but the essence of the house was sound. It was now secure, watertight, and hers. She kept saying this over and over in head. *The house is mine, it's mine. All mine.* Her new home, thanks to her Great Aunt Lily Anne and her Captain. Whoever he was, which Rose was determined to find out, she could honour his memory and restore his house as he would have liked it, with a few modern amenities of course.

Thirty-Three

Rose fell asleep in the armchair as the events of the day finally caught up with her. She fell into a deep, dreamless sleep.

The house went about its business around her. The candlelight flickered as the dusk faded into the dark. The shadows plotted a course around their sleeping companion. The house was peaceful and the air warm and tranquil, but full of the pungent smell of tobacco smoke. The quiet inhalation and exhalation of air as tobacco was smoked through a pipe. The faint outline of one of the shadows getting clearer and more defined.

The house was in darkness when Rose awoke with a start. She did not have a clue where she was. She could not make out anything familiar in her surroundings in the blackness. The moon was giving a milky sheen to the darkness and, very slowly, Rose made out the shape of the bed, surrounded by a sea of boxes. She shifted her body weight in the armchair, and something fell on her, making her scream and she leapt to her feet. She stumbled in the darkness for what seemed like an age, before her hands felt the light switch. Her fingers snapped the light on. The room was flooded with light and she looked down to see what it was that fell on her, just a moment ago. Of course, it had to be the sailors coat that she fell asleep resting her head on. Was it the Captain was making his presence felt yet again?

Rose was stiff and sore from her sleep. She stretched her body this way and that way, to try and ease away the aches. Her eyes looked across at the window and she was disappointed to see that she had forgotten to bring any curtains to cover the large expanse of window. She felt very exposed and wished she had thought of curtains before now. She could see glimpses of the cars going pass in the lane, so she knew that she could be seen from the lane too. The overgrown apple trees and shrubs in the garden were shielding her from view, but she still felt very exposed. Rose shivered as she remembered the trail of sand and wished she had invited a guest to keep her company on her first night in the house. She wished she had not been so hasty to let everyone go that afternoon.

There was no curtain pole or anything to drape something over to cover the window, so she turned on the light on the landing and switched off the bedroom light, leaving the bedroom door ajar. Perhaps she would take the mattress off the bed and put it in the back bedroom and sleep there on the floor.

Rose ventured downstairs and crept into the kitchen. The kitchen work surfaces still had the debris of the afternoon's activities. Dirty mugs and plates. Empty packets of cakes, crisps, and other goodies were littered across the worktop. She sighed and got to work, clearing up. Her phone was on the wooden windowsill and it vibrated to indicate that she had a message. She picked up the phone and looked. She had several, a couple from Steve and one from Val. They all wanted her to know that she only had to call them if she needed them anytime. The most recent one was from Mike. Mike was letting her know that he was popping back to the UK for a brief visit and wanted to see her to update her on his brilliant business acumen. He was asking her to confirm a date. Rose dropped the phone back down on the work surface and took a deep breath. Oh, my goodness, she thought, what bad timing.

Rose made herself a cup of tea and took it into the back room, overlooking the river to think. She cupped the mug in her hands and gazed across the river into the darkness beyond. She fancied she could hear the sea and sat down on the window seat. She had not switched the light on and was sitting in the semi darkness, with just the light of the hallway and kitchen. She glimpsed a man walking his dog and recognised them as Mickey and Bert. They were picking their way along the path; years of use meant that they both knew their way and did not need a torch. She waved at them, but they did not see her at the window and continued walking.

She could hear that sound of running water and at first thought that she had left the tap running in the kitchen. It was the sound of the river which was so close to the house. The water level was quite high, as there had been plenty of springtime rain. Rose had never heard it so loud before, but it did not worry her unduly as the sound of running water made her think once again of the Captain. She noted that she was once again sitting down next to the Captain's clothing, upstairs with his coat and downstairs with his hat. It was as if she was gleaning comfort from them, as she was all alone in the house for the first time at night. The comforting smell of tobacco not far away.

After a quick bite to eat, a sandwich and the last piece of Val's Victoria sponge, she took herself back upstairs to contemplate her sleeping arrangements. She wanted to sleep in the old brass bed, so tried to forget the glaring emptiness of the unadorned window and made the bed, with her new duvet set and Lisa's new pillows. She added a cosy knitted blanket and surveyed her work from the end of the bed. She was pleased with the result. She had not got around to getting a replica eiderdown for the bed yet, but the new duvet set was resplendent with big, bright roses and was the nearest she could find.

As much as she tried, she could not forget the fact that she had no curtains, so she pulled the armchair in front of the window. It did not cover all the expanse but did fill the majority. She would get changed for bed in the bathroom when she had turned the light off though!

Thirty-Four

Steve was back at the house bright and early the following day, but Rose was already up, washed and dressed. Rose answered the door with a bowl of cereal in one hand and a spoon in the other and motioned him to come in.

"Well, you certainly look at home!" he taunted with a wry smile.

"I hope you have not got a work schedule for today," Rose retorted. "I am missing curtain rails or poles or whatever you call them. I had to get undressed and dressed in the bathroom last night."

"I thought you would take control of the job when you moved in, I was not wrong," Steve replied.

Steve gestured for her to go upstairs. He patiently explained, "There were no curtains as they had found shutters at the windows, but they had taken them down to restore and the shutters were waiting in a shed outside for the plastering and painting to be finished."

Feeling slightly stupid, Rose looked once again at the window, there were no marks indicating that there were ever curtains hung there. She had not noticed that in her panic the night before.

They wandered into the back room and grabbed the sail cloth that was wrapped around the figurehead. It was thick and would not let the light through. Steve suggested hanging it from a wooden beam that was just in front of the window. He could put some hooks in the beam and take them out afterwards, when the shutters were replaced.

It seemed like a good compromise. As Steve went to get his tool box, Rose looked once again at the cloth. It was shaped like a ship's sail and even had holes set into the cloth itself. Perhaps this was an actual sail from the Captain's ship.

Her phone vibrated in her pocket, interrupting her thoughts. She fished it out and looked at the display. Another text from Mike, this one not so nice in tone and suggesting that she get back to him with a date, or he would not be able to fit her into his busy schedule. What a cheek, perhaps Rose would not be able to fit him in. She was still staring at the display in horror when Steve took it out of her hands. "Not sure who or what this is, but this is your first proper day in your new house. That look on your face is not welcome ..."

Rose readily agreed, "You are so right."

They set to, hanging the sail on the beam and sorting out the first problem of the day. Rose intentionally left her phone on one of the boxes and then forgot about it for the rest of the day.

The day was busy as she was trying to settle in, opening all the boxes and trying to work out if the contents were safe to come out yet or whether she should store them in the outbuildings. She kept out of the way of Steve, James, and George, but made them plenty of hot drinks. She ate her lunch in the garden, sitting on the bench in the warm sunshine, trying to identify which plants and trees were growing in her garden. The roses were easy to see by the large thorns on the stems. The fruit trees had blossomed already, so she had some clue there. The bulk of the garden was taken up by roses, the boundary hedge was made up of yew and a rambling rose. She could not help herself from inspecting every plant and she thoroughly enjoyed her afternoon in the sunshine, pottering about in the garden. Her skin felt quite tender when she went back indoors as she had caught the sun.

The men teased her for sunbathing when they were doing all the hard work, until they looked at her arms, which were scratched to pieces as she had investigated all the roses. Her hands were black with dirt and grime and were far dirtier than any of the men who had been working in the house all day.

"Hey Steve, do you know of a gardener or anyone that could help me tame the wilderness to keep me occupied, while you guys are working on the interior of the house?"

"Yeah, I know plenty, but they are already booked up solid for the summer."

The lads were all off to the pub that very evening, so they said they would ask around and see if they could find anyone else. Rose was asked if she would like to go with them, but she just wanted to be left alone in the house for a while.

As she saw the lads out, the conversation continued in the garden. Steve pointed out the many roses, James pointed out the fruit trees, and George identified the yew trees that stood in every corner of the garden. None of them could help with anything else slightly botanical. As the teasing and banter grew louder and louder, a voice was heard from over the hedge from the direction of the riverside footpath.

"Maybe I can help with the gardening problems?" interjected the male voice.

They all waited for the person to appear through the gap in the hedge and, sure enough, a man poked his head into the gap. Rose was amazed to see her handsome mystery man appear just a few inches from her face. She stepped back and stuck her hands in her pockets to stop her waving them about in excitement. Her thoughts ran away with her, he was real, not a ghost or anything sinister. Flesh and blood and a spectacular specimen at that! She adapted a defensive pose and stood with her feet apart and appraised the stranger with interest. Steve looked at her sideways, immediately noticing that something was amiss.

"Come through into the garden and see for yourself," Rose found herself saying, without thinking. The man then joined them in the garden and Rose could then see all of him. He was definitely the handsome mystery man that waved at her all those months ago. Rose was tempted to ask him if he remembered her, but before she could do so, he remarked, "You're the lady that I kept seeing at the window from the footpath. I hope I didn't startle you when I waved, but it seemed the most natural thing to do at the time. You know, I was not sure if you were real or a ghost!"

Thirty-Five

Rose could not believe that her mystery man remembered her as she did him. It had been ages since she had last spied him walking the footpath when Lisa was visiting. The first time, when he had waved at her, was months ago, she was touched that he had not forgotten her. Now, he was standing in front of her, waiting for her to speak.

Steve and the others did not know the man either. It turned out that all Rose had to do was to stand and listen for a while as the men struck up a conversation. She found out that the man's name was Tom and he had been a regular visitor to the Kent coast since he was a boy. He used to stay up at the caravan site a few miles away, but his family always visited this beach. They used to park in the lay by just past the front of the Captain's House and used the footpath that runs alongside the river to get to the beach. His dad never wanted to pay the car park charges at the beach and was furious at the double yellow lines that started at least two miles away, forcing holiday makers to pay the exorbitant charges! Tom had always liked the house and its garden. Whenever he was in the area, he would take a walk along the footpath to check on it. He was delighted with the improvements that had been made to the house, and he agreed with Rose when he commented that he thought the wonky chimney added a sense of charm to the place.

Tom was a gardener by trade and worked all over the country. He particularly liked to tackle older gardens which were next to old properties and restore them to their former splendour. Rose had inadvertently found her gardener, but just as she was going to ask him for his card, Steve butted in, with a 'Never heard of you comment,' and Rose saw that he was looking out for her yet again. She also noted his look of mutinous jealousy as well.

Rose impulsively decided to ask Tom into the house for a cuppa to discuss the garden in more detail. As she formulated this into a coherent sentence, she firmly but gently shoved Steve and the others out of the garden.

"You know, the earlier you leave the more drinking time you will have." Reluctantly, they all drove off and it was just Tom and Rose.

Rose was suddenly shy and busied herself making the tea. Tom leaned up against the worktop and continued to chat about the house and what it was like when he first saw it as a boy.

He said, "Everyone said it was haunted by an old sea captain, but I always saw a pretty lady amongst the flowers in the garden. The rest of my family could never see her when they were with me, just me. I was always drawn to the garden because, in the summer months, it was full of colourful flowers and was so inviting. I never properly set foot into the garden until now, because I was always worried about the ghostly old Captain as a boy! As an adult, I was worried about trespassing and getting into trouble with the owner. Now I know the owner, I guess I am not so worried now."

Rose said, "I think I know the ghostly captain too by now. He seems a friendly chap to me, but he doesn't seem to hang around long enough for us to have a conversation!"

Rose loved listening to Tom talk about the house and his stories of the Captain and was very interested to hear all about the lady that he had seen with the flowers. They wandered back out to the garden and sat down together on the bench cradling their mugs of tea in their hands and continued to chat.

Tom adored the garden, and this was evident in his conversation. "There are some old varieties of rose in this garden. They've been severely neglected. You might need to replace some of them. Some detective work might be required to work out what the garden used to be, but it could all be done by someone who knows what they are doing."

Tom was very knowledgeable about the garden, which was to be expected as he was a professional gardener. A gardener by trade. The garden was predominantly a rose garden and Tom would be very happy to guide her in renovating the garden to match the house. Rose was intending to contract out some of the heavy and monotonous garden work, but hearing Tom speak so eloquently about the roses she decided to work on the garden herself and ask Tom to help her. She was conscious that Tom might think that this was a way to avoid paying him for his services. Rose was not sure how to work this one out. This paled into insignificance when Tom remarked, "How about we continue this conversation later, can I take you out for dinner?"

Rose found herself answering, "Yeah, I would love to go out for dinner. Give me an hour and call back here. I will be ready."

Tom handed her his empty mug and left the way he had entered, waving as he left the garden.

Oh, my goodness, Rose thought. What have I done, just an hour to get ready when everything I own in is packed up in boxes! Rose went back inside the house and started to look for her phone. She had to text Lisa her news and get ready for a date. She remembered, after searching high and low downstairs and entering the bedroom, that it was there that she had left her phone. She ignored, for the second time, the text from Mike. She texted Lisa with her good news and the phone rang instantly. Lisa was on the line, giggling and teasing Rose, "OMG girl, the mystery man is real then, you are going out on a date, really? What is he like? He hasn't got a wife and a dozen kids then?" Lisa laughed.

Rose laughed with her friend, "You know I didn't ask, we just chatted about the garden and the vintage roses that Tom reckons grew here."

"The only Rose, Tom is interested in, is you, Rose. Let's face it, girly."

Rose kept her on the phone while she rummaged in the boxes and found her outfit for the evening. The friendly banter kept her nerves at bay. She was so excited and could hardly believe her luck. It was only when she looked at the time, she realized that she only had fifteen minutes to get ready. She immediately rang off, after promising to give Lisa an update in the morning, and ran into the bathroom like a demented headless chicken.

She looked at her reflection in the bathroom mirror that she had propped up on the windowsill. She caught a glimpse of the figurehead. She could have sworn that she was looking out of the window not inwards, but she could see her eyes and she was smiling straight at her. When she had finished her makeup, she made her way to the back bedroom and sure enough the figurehead was looking out towards the beach. Perhaps she was imagining things. Rose did not have the time for this. She could not tear her eyes away from the reflection, she felt the hairs on the back of her neck stand on end and it seemed as if time stood still. Suddenly, she heard a sharp 'rat a tat tat' on the front door and ran down the stairs to open it. She did not open it wide, as she was still unnerved by the spooky events in the bathroom but peered around the door like a little mouse. She saw that it was Tom and flung the door open wide.

He had changed and put a blue T-shirt on with a fresh pair of jeans. He was wearing a pair of brown loafers, polished to a shine. His T-shirt matched his blue eyes, which regarded Rose with an easy appreciation of her outfit, which had been put together on the go as well. Tom was tall, slim, and had a close-cropped head of brown hair. His complexion was tanned as he spent most of his time outside. He reached for Rose's hands and grasped them to draw her out of the house and into the garden.

He did not have a car waiting outside, but his work van still had the engine running. It was painted green with a logo on the side, a trellis design with a rose rambling across it.

Thirty-Six

Tom had booked a table for dinner at the Smugglers along the coast. A popular, busy place, intimate with cosy tables, crisp white table linen and candles. They were both dressed casually but were still greeted with a smile by the proprietor who knew Tom by name. This was Joe, Tom's brother, and it was his restaurant. Tom was staying above the restaurant with Joe for the summer and was looking for work locally.

Rose and Tom spent a pleasurable evening together. Rose was initially very shy but came out of her shell with Tom's attentiveness to her needs. He continually made her laugh and smile and she was reassured by his easy-going company. It was so nice to be herself and not have to think about anything too difficult. It was nice to get away from the Captain's House for a while. It had occupied her for months and all her conversation seemed to be fixated on the house. All her new friends were connected to the house in some way. She noted that she had leaned on Steve rather too much and she would have to sort that out soon, without hurting his feelings. She found herself discussing all of this with Tom.

When Tom and Rose found themselves the only ones left in the restaurant, his brother Joe brought out some coffee and biscuits for them. Joe joined them at the table and started to rib his brother about his love for old gardens, especially roses. Tom continued to speak with passion despite the teasing from his brother.

"I love looking for old roses, the true old-fashioned varieties. My favourite is the 'Jacobite Rose', an ancient, classical rose with white creamy double flowers. It lives almost indefinitely, renewing its growth constantly and it grows wild, but often marks the spot where a dwelling once was."

Joe explained, "This is the rose that is depicted on Tom's van in the logo. This is the rose that Tom looks for. It helps him find those old gardens that have been lost. Sometimes, the owners of such gardens want Tom's help to restore the gardens to their former splendour. Others just rip the gardens out and replace them with a concrete hard standing to park their cars!" Tom added, "I offer to dig out the old plants that they don't want and take cuttings to sell on, not always roses. You would be surprised how much garden plants and other garden features get thrown away, that can be recycled and make me a profit!"

Tom smiled at Joe, explaining to Rose how his business worked and his passion for roses. He caught Rose's eye and she blushed, a deep crimson red. Joe read the signals and chuckled quietly to himself and then left them alone, retreating to the kitchen. It was very late when they left and returned to the Captain's House.

On the way back to the house, Rose explained, "I have only spent one night in the house, since I had bought it, and that was last night. I am a bit nervous as we are returning so late. I don't think that I have left any lights on at all in the house."

The house loomed out of the darkness when they drew up the driveway.

"Give me the keys and I will unlock the door and put some lights on for you," Tom suggested. Rose did not need asking twice and handed the keys to him and watched as he approached the front door. He opened the door and reached inside to switch the hall and porch light on. He stumbled on something on the front door mat, which grumbled and let out a small feeble cry. The light illuminated a small furry mass on the doorstep, which was now making the most awful racket. Rose rushed out of the van and into the porch, kneeling down to get a closer look. Rose picked up the bundle of fur and cuddled it tightly. It was a black and white kitten, barely old enough to be away from its mother. Rose looked out into the garden for the mother cat, but there was nothing there. Tom held the door open wide and they took the cat into the living room and placed the kitten in the Captain's armchair. The unexpected arrival looked hungry. Rose found a saucer and put a tiny amount of watered-down milk in it and placed it next to the kitten on the chair. The kitten lapped the milk furiously and, when it was all gone, nudged at Rose's hand for some more. Rose knew that she should not offer too much food at once and was not even sure she should have even given it milk, albeit the watered-down variety. She scooped it up for another cuddle. Tom had placed an old newspaper that he had found while she was feeding the cat by the back door already. It was as if he knew she would not turn the animal away.

It was past midnight and very late, but Tom filled and flicked the switch on the kettle. Tom made his way back into the living room and sat down on the window seat next to the Captain's hat.

He looked across at Rose, cuddling the kitten, "You have found your company now and someone to welcome you when you come home. What are you going to call him, or is it a her?"

Rose noticed that it was a male cat and remarked that, "I will call him Mowzer, after the famous Mousehole cat from Cornwall." She recounted the Cornish legend to Tom, about another Tom, a fisherman who went fishing on Christmas Eve to bring home a catch for the starving folk of Mousehole. His cat, a black and white cat called Mowzer, went out fishing with him and sang with the storm cat to bring the bad weather to a close and enable them to return to harbour safely with the fish.

As Rose told the story, a very sleepy kitten made its way to Tom and, after a cuddle, curled up in the Captain's hat and fell fast asleep. Rose followed the kitten and she sat at Tom's feet, looking up at him. Tom reached down and drew her to him, and they shared a shy kiss together on the window seat. The house felt serene and still. Rose and Tom left Mowzer curled up in the Captain's hat and made their way upstairs.

When they got upstairs, Rose stopped in the doorway of the bedroom, suddenly nervous. She had never felt like this with anyone before and usually took things so slowly that the new man in her life got bored of waiting and went off with someone else. This was different. She felt different. There was an urgency to get intimate with Tom and get to know him properly. Tom slide his arm around her shoulders and gently pushed her towards the bed, lowering his head so his lips could reach hers and he could kiss her slowly as he did so. They tumbled onto the bed and she giggled as he almost crushed the life out of her in his eagerness to get to know her, mirroring her emotions exactly.

They took their clothes off quickly. Hands fumbling with buttons, clasps, and zips, until they were both naked. Their hands explored each other, fingers running across bare skin. Fingertips causing ripples of excitement to bubble on the surface of their skin. Their breath becoming faster and more ragged. Rose gasped as Tom's lips moved from hers. He started to kiss her neck then continued to kiss her, while moving slowly down her body. She rose up underneath him, wanting more, and reached out to touch him and kiss him in the same way. She did not start with his lips, but somewhere much more intimate. Tom groaned involuntary as she did so. They kissed, teased, and stroked each other until neither of them could take it anymore. Their bodies merged into one. It was very late, when Rose and Tom finally curled up together to sleep. Before she fell asleep, she felt contented and truly happy in her new home for the first time since she moved in.

The roof tiles of the house took on a milky sheen in the moonlight and shadows abounded in the garden. The garden was full of light and dark. Shadows fell awkwardly, leaving abstract shapes on the driveway and the unkempt lawn.

The night was silent, but within the garden and the house itself the sound of the sea could be heard. Not the faint sounds of the waves on the shingle shore, but louder, much much louder. It was as if the ocean was all around the house. The waves sounded loud and clear, as if they were crashing into the stern of a ship. The air was moist and salty and everywhere was dripping wet as if there had been a recent shower, not a dry, warm day.

Nighttime creatures were avoiding the garden and could be seen scurrying along the boundaries, but not crossing into the garden, for the garden seemed to take on a life of its own. The grasses were moving from side to side and the shrubs were shaking from their roots upwards. The only stillness in the garden were the roses, standing still and serene amidst the movement. On the largest of the rose bushes, a white rose gleamed a virginal white in the middle of the garden and the shadows grew longer and longer. The smell of the sea was overwhelming, but powerful.

Shadows could be seen at the windows of the house. Lamps

appeared in all the windows, shining brightly out into the darkness, adding a golden glow to the colours that were unfolding in the night. Curtains and drapes glimmered in the brightness, so the interlocking rose design was clear.

The front door sprung open, to reveal the Captain's coat hanging on the bannister at the bottom of the stairs. There were lamps lit in the kitchen, shining a bright light in the direction of the sea itself. The door did not emit its familiar squeak, but opened quietly, so so quietly. No one in the house stirred, not Tom or Rose. Mowzer twitched an ear and rubbed his face with his paw, as if he was waving. The kitten opened an eye sleepily and started to purr.

Surprisingly, the bench was upright, but appeared to be bobbing gently as if it was on the deck of a boat. Two shapes started to appear together sitting on the bench. They were vague and could just be seen as the mist started to roll in from the sea.

The stream bubbled gently and gurgled as the water started to flow quicker across the smooth pebbles of the riverbed. The mist grew thicker and thicker until the house was hidden from anything that might have sought entry. It was if the house was protecting itself and cloaking its occupants from the outside world.

Thirty-Seven

They were awoken by a scampering at the end of the bed and a small furry head in their faces, an indignant Mowzer, who was hungry again and in need of another cuddle. Rose looked across at Tom by her side, tangled up in the bed covers with her. She grinned sheepishly when she recalled the events of the night. She was interrupted by the kitten that bounded onto Tom's head and started licking his ear. Rose peeled the cat off his ear and took him back downstairs for another saucer of milk. She then returned to the bedroom for some clothes. She was amazed that she was wandering around the house naked with a man she had just met waiting for her in her bed. Although, she was not that brazen to return to the bedroom with nothing on and went into the bathroom for her dressing gown which was hanging on the back of the door.

It was still very early and the sailcloth that was acting as a makeshift curtain was keeping the morning light out of the room. Tom had gone back to sleep and looked adorable with a hint of morning stubble on his chin. She climbed back into bed and his arm reached out for her and pulled her close to him. She curled up against him, mirroring his position and drifted back to sleep.

It was not early when Steve arrived a couple of hours later. They both sat up with a start as they heard his knock on the door. Mowzer arrived at the end of the bed, looking frightened at the unexpected loud noise that had awoken him from his slumber. Rose pulled her dressing gown tight around her and called out for him to let himself in with his key.

She looked at Tom and said, "How am I going to explain this one?"

She need not have worried as Mowzer was down the stairs before her. He fell down the last stair and landed on Steve's feet in a untidy heap as he came through the doorway and into the hall.

Steve looked down and back up at Rose, "I see you have a guest."

"Oh, yes. This is Mowzer, he was on the doorstep last night. Do you like him?" she replied.

"Yes, the kitten is very cute, as are you, but I was referring to your other guest, Tom, as his van is outside!" Rose blushed a deep crimson red and picked up Mowzer and cuddled him, in front of her face to shield her from Steve's gaze. She did not have time to reply as Tom appeared at the top of the stairs, fully dressed, with a rather smug grin as he called out a cheery, "Good morning."

Steve was flabbergasted but did not say anything untoward to Rose. He could not believe his eyes. He did not want to believe that Rose had spent the night with Tom, after all he had done for her. Steve had planned the softly, softly approach and it had failed dismally. He had not managed to get Rose to go out on another date with him, but he had planned to ask her again very soon. Steve wondered what Tom had that he did not. Rose sensed Steve's displeasure and was upset that she had caused it. She was not the type to go to bed with a man on a first date, but it had just happened, and it felt right.

Tom came downstairs and made his way to the kitchen and Steve joined him. Rose decided to make a tactical retreat and left the men talking in the kitchen and made her way upstairs to get dressed. When she returned, Tom had left. Steve was in the outbuilding mixing up some plaster for the walls. She realised that she did not have Tom's number or any way of contacting him again. She followed Mowzer into the living room, she found Tom's business card in the Captain's hat on the armchair. He had written his personal mobile number on the other side and without thinking it through she texted him straight away – 'thank you for a lovely evening'. When her brain was once more in gear, she worried that she had been too hasty in replying, but on receiving a reply from Tom almost immediately echoing the same sentiments she was reassured. Tom's text was short, but full of intrigue; 'thank you, we must do that again very soon'.

Steve bustled in, covering the armchair with a dust sheet and handing her the Captain's hat without saying a word. Rose knew that she was not forgiven and went into the garden. She caught sight of the roses and thought again of the white rose that had been discussed at length the previous evening. How clever, to be able to see where a cottage would have been by the garden that had been left behind. She could not wait to start the garden with Tom and find out more about all the roses in the Captain's garden. She was sure that she had lots of the old roses that Tom had talked about last night. She would have to take Tom to 'The Ship to show him the painting of the garden. Perhaps the lady that Tom had seen in the garden as a boy when he used to walk along the footpath to the beach with his family was the mistress of the house in years gone by, the lady who the figurehead was modelled on. Or it could have been her Great Aunt Lily. It would be so interesting to find out. Although it didn't make sense as the lady of the figurehead belonged to a different era, so perhaps the Captain's house was haunted after all.

Before she could call him, she felt a now familiar tugging at the bottom of her jeans. Mowzer was hungry again. Rose took the complaining Mowzer back into the house and shut the door. She told

Steve that she was going out and she made her way into the village to the local shops for some cat food.

In the village, Rose made some enquiries about the kitten at the local vets, but the kindly receptionist told her that she was not aware of any pregnant cats or new kittens in the village but did recall some feral cats living in the outbuildings of the Captain's House for a while. Rose made an appointment for Mowzer to see the vet later in the afternoon to be checked out and gathered some leaflets on kitten care.

Thirty-Eight

When Rose got back to the Captain's House, she found everyone hard at work plastering the walls and repairing the wooden panels in the riverside room. It was all coming together, and she would soon have two liveable and finished rooms downstairs. It was exciting, but she could feel an uncomfortable atmosphere. It was obvious that Steve was disgruntled by the fact that he had found Tom at the house this morning. Rose was very keen to make things right with Steve as he meant the world to her, just not in the way that he wanted.

She hovered for a while, making sure that she was getting in Steve's way, so eventually he yelled, "What is the matter with you? Why are you just hovering right there? You are so in my way!" She was startled by his yell, she expected him to moan, but not to shout.

Rose retorted, "I needed to get your attention, can we have a chat?"

Steve followed Rose into the kitchen and they both leaned against the opposite sides of the kitchen walls, creating a physical division. It was crazy, two good friends glaring from each side of the room at each other. Rose was mortified by the turn of events. She gasped audibly at the incredulous scene. This was enough for Steve to realise that Rose did not intend to upset him. She was just as worried about their friendship as he was. However, Steve was not going to make the first move and he just waited, with his arms folded across his chest, for Rose to speak.

Rose started to formulate the right words, but then stepped across and hugged Steve first. She looked up at him and grinned.

"You know what a good friend you are to me and how much I value your friendship and advice. Going out with Tom just sort of happened. We went to a delightful little restaurant called the Smugglers and I met his brother Joe. Tom told me all about his gardening business and he has offered to help me with the garden."

She skipped some of the later detail and tried to explain how evening panned out. How it just felt so right and how she did not engage her brain until the morning, until Steve had knocked on the door.

Steve shook his head from side to side as he tried to comprehend what she meant. He knew then, that he had missed his chance with Rose and he should have made his feelings known earlier, instead of just assuming Rose wanted to play the 'long game' as well.

It was nice to clear the air and when James and George entered the kitchen to grab a cool drink from the fridge, Rose and Steve were still standing very close.

"So pleased you two have made up. Steve's has been like a bear with a sore head all morning," James said. "Has it got something to do with that Tom guy then?" James went on. Rose was secretly pleased that Steve had not told James and George about the night's events and his discovery of Tom at the house in the morning. She knew he must have been tempted to gossip with his mates while they were working.

"Tom and I went out last night to the Smugglers, and I met his brother Joe. Tom told me all about his gardening business and we had a lovely time." She looked down at her feet as she finished her sentence and did not catch Steve's eye.

As she looked down, a now familiar face looked back. A furry black and white one with large ears, just like a bat. Mowzer was hungry yet again and scrambling up her legs, then up her torso onto her shoulder. He was just getting ready to bite her ear when she grabbed him and gave him a cuddle. She nodded her head at Steve in the direction of the bag, containing all her recent cat purchases. He reached into the bag and took out Mowzer's new bowls and a pouch of kitten food. Mowzer leapt from her shoulder to the floor and started to wind himself around Steve's legs. Mowzer was not fussy about who fed him and seemed to seek attention wherever he could find it.

Rose and Steve prepared Mowzer's first proper meal together and watched as he devoured it in sixty seconds flat. James and George laughed.

"That cat will eat you out of house and home. Are you sure you want it?"

Rose laughed, "A house is not a home without a cat," she said. "The house did not feel so empty and lonely with Mowzer here last night."

Steve just shrugged his shoulders with a wry smile, biting his lip to stop him making an inappropriate wisecrack and letting James and George in on the events of the previous night. Rose blushed as she realised what she had just said. Steve led Rose out of the kitchen before she could say any more, shaking his head once more.

Mowzer skidded round their feet and raced into the room and darted from wall to wall. He ran up the armchair and on and off the window seat at high speed, until the branches from the bush outside started tapping the glass on the window. The wind was picking up and all the trees and shrubs were blowing in the ever-strengthening gale. Mowzer stood on his hind legs, transfixed with the movement.

He had his paws in the Captain's hat and it seemed like he was taking charge of the ship, steering it into the weather. James came into the room with a radio in his hands. "Storm's brewing," the announcer was saying, "baton down the hatches tonight."

Rose gathered Mowzer in her arms and slid him gently into the newly purchased cat basket. He whined loudly as she shut the wire door. He leaned against the wire, meowed pitifully, and pushed his little body against the wire. Rose picked up the box and carried it to her car. She placed the box carefully on the front seat and then pulled at the seat belt to make it big enough to wrap around the box and keep him safe, giggling at herself for being so daft! When Mowzer was all plugged in, she drove Mowzer to the vets as quickly as she could. His cries were getting harder to ignore. She turned on the radio to drown out the sound of his cries. She was very pleased not to encounter any traffic on the way.

When she opened the door to the vets, she was surprised to see that it was empty apart from the receptionist that she had met earlier in the day. She expected it to be busy as it she had taken the last available appointment.

"Hello, my dear. Back again with that noisy fella this time, bring him over to the counter so that I can have a good look at what is making all of the racket."

"Well, he does not like being confined, but he is a lovely, little kitten normally. Not quite as vocal."

The receptionist grinned at Rose and replied, "Most cats hate coming to the vets, but I have not heard a meow that loud from such a little one for a while. I love his black and white markings. What have you called him again?"

"I have called him Mowzer, after the famous Mousehole cat. Have you heard the Cornish story?"

"Yes, I have, we have been to Cornwall on our annual holidays for years and we always stay in a lovely house in Newquay on the harbourside. I know all about the Mousehole cat, I am sure I have a children's book about a cat from Mousehole somewhere in the house. A black and white cat too. I see the resemblance from the story. What a handsome fella, your Mowzer is. He is going to grow into a real handsome cat. Hope he quietens down a bit though, he is beginning to give me a headache! You're the lady from our Captain's House, aren't you? No wonder, you called him Mowzer. A brilliant name. Fantastic."

The door behind the receptionist opened and a tall, lanky man held it open for a very smartly dressed woman, holding a lead with a very small greyish-white poodle attached. The dog was whining and strained at his lead, eager to get away. The lady was dragged toward the exit door, pulling against the lead to stop the poodle dragging her as well. Rose glanced at the lady's face and recognised her as Phyliss from the antique shop.

Phyliss had recognised her immediately and stopped when she was alongside Rose. She gave a sharp tug on the lead and yelled 'Porridge' at the top of her voice. Porridge stopped instantly and dropped with a whine to the floor and looked back imploringly at her owner. She was desperate to get out of there and was going to try every trick in the book.

"Don't take any notice of Porridge, my dear. She is good at looking pathetic. She is not even ill, just come in for her jabs. How are you, my dear? Feeling better, are you? You were rather poorly when I saw you last. You bought the telescope, didn't you? I haven't seen you around the village since then. I was getting worried about you. Now, Val said, when I met her in one of the shops, that you are the lady that inherited that old spooky house up the lane there. Surely not, you look like you would have one of the new apartments by—"

Mowzer gave an almighty meow at being ignored for so long and interrupted Phyllis's flow, cutting her short mid-sentence. Porridge looked up at the counter and then crawled along the floor on her belly and when she reached Phyliss hid behind her legs. Everyone gathered around the animal carrier and peered in at Mowzer, who angrily peered out and meowed again.

"We better get you inside before you get any angrier, mate," the tall lanky guy said, grabbing the handle of the box with one hand and opening the door with the other. He ushered Rose into the clinical space of the consultation room and shut the door behind him.

"That will stop you having to answer any of her questions, won't it? Our Phyliss is a very sweet woman, but so nosey you would not believe. What she doesn't know she finds out from everyone else. She is a bit like our very own Miss Marple. Without the murder of course!"

He brandished his hand to Rose to formally greet her and smiled.

"I am the local vet, Dale, and I am very pleased to meet you."

He was casually dressed in jeans and a T-shirt, underneath a blue vets' tunic with a name badge pinned onto the front. Rose guessed that he was the owner of the practice, He was an older man with white-grey hair. She reckoned he was in his sixties. She wondered if it was him that caused Phyliss to rattle out all the questions without taking a breath as he was not wearing a wedding ring.

Dale saw her glance down at his hands and laughed.

"You are so right; I am sure I know what you are thinking. It was me. I think Phyliss has had a crush on me for some time. Please don't tell anyone. I find it very amusing as I am gay and totally not a suitable match for our Phyliss. Enough about me, what about this little guy in here. Is he friendly?"

"Oh yes, he is very friendly, I think he wants out of the box! He arrived unexpectedly on my doorstop and I think he is a stray. I really want to keep him. I need you to check that he is healthy and tell me what I need to know about vaccinations and things, please."

Dale laughed and reached inside the box and grabbed an indignant Mowzer and gave him a cuddle. He gently put him on the table and Mowzer sat down and gazed at the pair of them before licking his paw and proceeded to have a wash.

"He's a cocky little guy, isn't he? Not a care in the world now he is out of the box."

Dale gave Mowzer a quick look over, listened to his heart, looked into his eyes, ears, mouth, and gave him a thorough once over and then gave him his first vaccination. He also added a microchip. Mowzer was not happy with this turn of events and, after being jabbed, turned tail and made his way back to his box. Hunkering down at the back. Peering out mournfully at Rose.

Dale and Rose went back into the waiting room, hoping that Phyliss had departed and had not hung about to speak with Rose. Vera, the receptionist, grinned at the pair of them.

"Yes, she has gone. She took a fair bit of persuading. I just told her that you were finishing up early tonight and hinted that you were going to the Quiz Night at the village hall with the rest of the team. She has rushed off to get herself beautiful, as the antique ahop has a team too."

Rose stifled a giggle and grinned at Dale, "That means she has forgotten all about me and my telescope. Thank you so much. How much do I owe you?"

Vera smiled at Rose and retorted, "You need to pay for the check up and vaccinations, but encouraging Phyliss to leave, without checking on you, is totally free!"

Rose signed up to a Lifelong Healthcare plan for Mowzer, paying with her credit card which she carried with her mobile phone. Her phone trilled, just as she was putting her card away. She had a text message from Steve. 'The house should hold up against the storm, but I will come over if need me. Just call.'

"Have you heard the news about the big storm on its way tonight?" Rose informed Dale and Vera.

"Oh yes, the big storm in the village hall when we win, or the weather?"

"The weather, I reckon," she responded as the external door smashed open and a figure bent double against the wind and rain fell into the surgery with a dog. They both stood there dripping before shaking vigorously all over the floor. Rose took this opportunity to leave and sneaked out of the door and into the weather.

Thirty-Nine

When Rose arrived back at the house and released Mowzer from his basket, she filled a litter tray for Mowzer so she could keep him inside and safe during the storm. She had noted on her way inside that the men had made sure that all their tools and materials were packed away safely in the outbuildings before they went home. They had even picked up the garden bench that was normally found on its back with its legs in the air in the mornings and put that in the outbuilding too. The guys had figured that Rose liked to sit there when they had all gone home, as the grass was flat and worn through in places. Steve had lit a fire in the grate, to test the chimney, but also to make the house cosy for Rose in the impending storm.

Rose was not seeing Tom that evening as he had already had other plans, so she knew that she was going to be alone. Everyone had bustled around her all afternoon and she was as prepared as she could ever be. She knew that Steve was concerned about her being alone. He had already told her that he was on the other end of the phone if she needed him at any time and he had texted her again at the surgery. She was pleased that she had cleared the air with Steve, and everything was OK between them now.

The night drew in and the darkness fell. The wind picked up and the house shook and trembled, bracing itself against the wind. Some of the window frames were rotten with gaps between the frames and the bricks. This made the wind whistle and scream. Mowzer, however, had a full stomach and was fast asleep in his very own Captain's hat on the window seat. Rose sat in the armchair and listened to the radio, tuned in to a local station. The music was modern and upbeat and was a direct contrast to the events the other side of the glass. It was keeping her mood positive, and she welcomed the distraction. She needed to get a television sorted, as well as broadband. The dream of living in an old property was all very well, but she was missing her soaps. She was rather partial to 'Neighbours' and 'Home and Away'. She had satellite television when she lived in town and wasted a lot of time watching the big American dramas, but she loved to watch them, and her TV Planner was always full.

Rose was sure that Steve had lost the plot earlier when he had set about lighting a fire in the grate to test the chimney. The chimney had been swept and Rose did not see the need at the time as the afternoon was warm and humid. She had to admit that he was right and that it was a good time to do it. There was nothing wrong with the chimney, they all knew that, as it was now standing tall and straight and not at the crazy angle that she had previously loved. The night was now cold. The wind was penetrating every corner of the house. She had a slow cooker going all day, with a beef casserole with vegetables inside. The meal had filled her up and she was feeling a little like Mowzer: warm, cosy and snug, not in the Captain's hat but in her very own Captain's house.

She had her phone beside her and it chimed to let her know that there was a message. Rose had not replied to Mike's earlier messages and hoped it was not another one from him. She had stepped away from him, when he left her for his business trip. She did not think of him as her boyfriend any more, but she had not told him yet. She knew she had not finished it properly and needed to do so very soon. The message was not from Mike, it was from Val asking how she was getting on with the storm and inviting her to take up one of her guest's rooms for the night to save her being alone in the house during the storm. Rose picked up her phone and rang her back, preferring to speak to her and secretly wanting her voice as company.

Val answered at the first ring, sounding alarmed as if something was already wrong. She was very worried about Rose being in the house all alone with the wind raging outside. Rose was starting to see her point but did not want to leave the house at the first sign of trouble. She changed the subject quickly by describing the new addition to her life. The kitten, not Tom. She was keeping Tom to herself for a while, as he seemed too good to be true. She knew that Steve and the guys knew about Tom, but she also knew they would not gossip about her. Val would only find out if she told her. They chatted for ages until Val was reassured that Rose would be fine. Val ended the call by stating that she would send her husband out whatever the weather if Rose needed him and he would take her back to The Lanterns.

The phone chimed again and again as the night wore on, her mum and dad, Lisa, Steve, and Tom all texted her because of the weather. She spent the evening merrily texting back, stating that she was fine. When she had finished all her texting, she popped another log on the fire, pulled the fire guard around the fire. When she stood up she glimpsed the surface of the river in which was reflected a fleeting glimpse of the moon from the window. The water was higher than she remembered or expected. She could hear the river water over the music on the radio. She padded into the kitchen and looked out of that window too. The water level was getting very high. Her first thought about the house all those months ago came back to haunt her and she wondered if the house really behaved like a ship and would float!

Forty

Rose was not sure whether to spend the night curled up in the armchair in front of the fire with Mowzer or to go to bed. She attempted to sleep in the chair but could not settle and ended up in bed. She snuggled up under the covers and could not help thinking about Tom again. The previous night felt a bit like a film scene; perfect and a bit too good to be true. She ran over the events of the that evening again and again in her mind. The wind was blowing up outside and then the rain started. It lashed against the windowpanes and made a frightful racket. She was joined by Mowzer, who was also disturbed by the rain, and they snuggled up together. Mowzer purred when he got cosy and that comforting noise lulled Rose to a deep sleep.

Her dreams were vivid, full of colour and full of the house. She was walking around the house, but the rooms kept changing and the scenes kept changing. The furnishings seemed familiar. The Captain was glimpsed as a shadowy figure always just ahead or just behind her, but even he kept changing. His clothes were different; his uniform, hat, and coat changing with the vivid colours of her dream. There were many Captains all from different centuries, always blending into a figure right there, but on the edge of Rose's dreams. Rose walked through a doorway next to a fireplace and continued her journey through a much bigger house, grander and more in keeping with a wealthy Captain. Then, her dream lost its colour and everything turned sepia, then black.

She lay still and was lost in her dreams for a while, before Mowzer's purring woke her. It was dawn and the room was bathed in a golden ethereal glow. Rose had not closed the makeshift curtain and the sunlight was causing a ripple effect on the ceiling. The ripples reminded Rose of water and she went to the window to look at the aftermath of the storm.

She looked out onto a different landscape. The garden was waterlogged, and parts of the garden were totally submerged. It looked like the river had burst its banks, so Rose rushed to the back of the house to be sure. She was right, the water level of the river was level with the banks and the floodwater surrounded most of the house. Looking out of the window she felt that she could drift out to sea at any minute, as the footpath and fields were under water too. Mowzer had come to find her and walked up and down the windowsill in front of her, keeping her company as she peered at saturated landscape below.

Downstairs was dry and not wet underfoot as Rose had expected and she felt foolish for rolling her jeans up before she ventured downstairs. She expected the house to be at least an inch or so underwater, by what she had seen outside from the upstairs windows. She explored all the downstairs room and there was no sign of any water in the house. All ship shape as you would expect a Captain's house to be. Opening the front door, she looked out and the floodwater started a couple of metres away from the front porch. Pulling on her wellies which were by the door, she ventured into the garden and walked around the house to the back where the house overlooked the river. The house was standing dry and clear of all the surrounding flood water. It was watertight, just like a boat. An island

172

in an ocean. It was as if the water was being repelled by the house.

Venturing back into the garden she saw that parts of the garden were flooded, sodden, and some areas uncannily just damp. It was strange and unnerving. The water, mud, and damp soil glistened in the sunlight and a slight damp haze was forming. Rose made her way to the gate and looked out onto the flooded lane. There was at least a foot of water on the other side of her hedge, and she wondered how The Lantern's had faired further up the lane.

A loud meow told her that Mowzer was out and about with her in the garden, and she raced to find him before he fell into a large puddle or something much deeper. He was waiting for her by the back-door step right at the edge of the dry land that was surrounding the house. He was not getting all his paws wet, but he could not resist dabbing at the water with one paw for fun. He was not impressed by the wetness of his fur when he had finished his games. They went back into the house together and Rose set about making breakfast for the two of them.

Rose spent the morning putting another meal in her slow cooker and playing with Mowzer, it was not until lunchtime that she realised that she had not had any phone calls, visitors, or company of any sort. It was a weekday, so the men would normally be at work on the house, but no one had turned up. There had been no traffic up or down the lane at all either. When she checked there was no signal on her mobile which explained her lack of calls.

She paced up the stairs into the room with the figurehead and was caught up in her expression once again. She stood very still and felt her hair raise up at the back of her neck. She felt her panic draining away to be replaced by a calm, tranquil feeling. Her mind drifted away with the overwhelming smell of dampness and water and she could have sworn that the floor ebbed and flowed with the tide. She was floating. The floor started to tilt like a boat and then, as abruptly as the sensation started, it stopped. The sound of the sea was replaced by what sounded like several voices talking at once.

Slowly and carefully, she made her way back downstairs, gripping the handrail for support. Everyone seemed to turn up at once. Steve arrived with Val in the passenger seat and, just as they were getting out the vehicle, Tom pulled up alongside them in his van.

Perfect timing. No more excuses. She would have to introduce Tom to Val, but before she could open her mouth, Val turned to Tom.

"Fancy seeing you here. I was not expecting you."

Tom walked up to Val and enveloped her in a big bear hug and smacked her cheek with a big slobbery kiss. "Auntie Val, always a pleasure to see you. Have you got any sweets in your pockets?"

Val returned his affection and held his face in his hands and looked deep into his eyes. "How old do you think you are, Tom? I stopped carrying sweets for little Tom in my pockets when you were eleven and you told me, in front of your brother, that you were too tough for sweets and all grown up. You still accept the sweets at Christmas, don't you?"

Rose stared at Val and then at Tom, "You know each other? I don't have to introduce you after all? Really? How come?"

"We have stayed with Auntie Val for our summer holidays for years. Our family were her first paying customers. I remember mum getting so excited that she was getting a discount and being able to stay in a newly renovated room with brand new everything."

"What a coincidence, as I was her first customer in the new annexe!"

Val interrupted the flow, "Very nice, but how do you both know each other?" Steve caught Rose's eye with a saucy grin and winked.

At that same moment, Val looked at Rose and caught the deep dark red blush that was spreading from her neck upwards. Rose looked at the floor and wished it to would open and swallow her. It was like watching a sex scene on the TV with her mum and dad in the room. So embarrassing.

"Oh, like that, is it. You two are together. Oh Rose, how nice. I thought you had the hots for Steve!"

Rose now held her head in her hands as well as looking at the floor. She thought it was embarrassing a moment ago and it was now ten times worse.

Forty-One

So, she turned everyone's attention back to the house.

Everyone was stunned that the house had not sustained any water damage as a result of the river bursting its banks. The floodwater had not reached the house at all. The house looked like a manor house surrounded by its own moat. Very quaint and picturesque in the sun. Tom was pleased that the house had not sustained any damage in the storm, but he was much more interested in the garden. The rose bushes were hardly waterlogged at all and some parts of the garden seemed to be not even damp. The wind and rain seemed to have rearranged the garden and pushed the soil into mounds in places.

Tom had wandered away from the discussions and was poking about in the garden with a large stick and muttering to himself.

Rose left Steve and Val making their way towards the house and joined Tom in the garden. He was standing where the bench used to be and scuffling about with his boot. There was something shiny in the dirt. He reached down and picked it out of the soil, wiping the object on his trouser leg to clean it. He handed it straight to Rose. It was a ring, that looked gold in colour. Two bands of gold were woven together to make a ring. Rose held it in the palm of her hand and the centre of her hand felt warm where the ring was resting. She picked it up with her finger and thumb and peered closely at it. It looked as if it had an inscription inside it, but it needed a proper clean. Tom and Rose went back to the kitchen and showed the ring to Val and Steve. Rose reached for a tea towel to wipe the residue mud from the ring and then raised it up to the light to make out the inscription. 'I venture across the seas, but always return to you.' There it was again, the same phrase as inscribed on the back of the bench. It was found in the same place where that bench had stood before it was put into the outbuilding for safety last night.

Rose handed the ring back to Tom and they passed the ring from person to person. It was quite heavy. The men seemed to think that it was a good quality ring by the fact that it was heavy. Rose did not care about the value. She just wanted them to hand the ring back to her, she had an irresistible urge to try it on. She almost snatched it from Tom as he handed it back to her and she slid it onto her ring finger on her right hand. It fitted perfectly, as if it was made for her. She gasped. Tom, who had been watching her intently, caught her hand and held it tightly. "Looks like it was made for you, Rose," he whispered.

Another car stopped in the lane outside, and people could be heard splashing about in the lane and coming up the drive. Rose stuck her right hand in her pocket to hide the ring. She went out into the garden to meet them.

Doreen appeared first and then Bob. Doreen waded through the water and stopped and stared when she noticed that the Captain's House was dry and standing proud of the water. She was still standing motionless when Rose joined her a couple of moments later. Doreen held a broom and roll of bin bags and was obviously expecting to help clear flood water from the house. The pub was flooded, and the water had covered the floors and filled the cellar. Doreen was amazed that the Captain's House had escaped the water as it was so close to the river. Bob was even more incredulous than Doreen and was making his way back to the car, stating, "I don't think we are needed here after all. Come on, love." Doreen was not so keen to leave and yelled back, "I've just arrived, I am not going yet, I will walk back." When she saw Steve and Tom she added, "If one of these lads take me back, they can have a pint on the house!"

Rose did not want to invite Doreen into the house but did not want to appear rude. She still was not sure if she trusted Doreen and knew that Doreen was not yet aware that Val was in the house already. Doreen then spotted Val and rushed across to her.

"Have The Lanterns escaped the floods?"

Val sounded more than a little smug when she replied that The Lanterns and the annexe Little Lanterns had escaped the flood entirely and the lane was totally clear of water at their end. She went on to say, as if to rub even more salt in the wound, that she had new guests that morning, journalists who were reporting on the floods who needed somewhere to stay."

Doreen looked downcast at this, "I have had to cancel my guests as the pub is flooded."

Her bottom lip trembled, and she held both hands to her face.

"Oh, I don't know what we are going to do," she went on, "we are already running out of ready cash, the bank won't give us anymore. We can't take on any more debt, as we cannot repay what we have got." She then burst into tears.

Forty-Two

Doreen recovered her composure reasonably quickly and was embarrassed by her outburst and the information that she had shared. Val was mortified by Doreen's change of circumstance as Doreen had arrived in the village a very wealthy woman after a large inheritance. Her situation was very similar to Rose's situation. They had both been new to the area and the village and had inherited property. Val wondered where Doreen's inheritance had all gone. She was sure that the pub had been doing well financially. It always seemed to be busy during the weekends but, then again, week days were always quiet.

It transpired that Val and Doreen had fallen out over the fact that Doreen started to take in paying guests at The Ship. She offered cut down rates and poached some of Val's customers by wooing them when they went into the pub to eat. Those customers went on to stay at The Ship the next time they visited. Val experienced a downturn in business for a while and it caused Doreen and Val to fall out in a big way.

It now dawned on Val why Doreen's behaviour changed and why she started offering bed, breakfast, and evening meals at The Ship. Doreen and Bob were only trying to make extra money as the pub was not paying its way.

Val was a kindly woman and had a very forgiving nature. She hugged Doreen close.

"Whatever has happened in the past is just that, in the past. I will do all I can to help." This resulted in the two women embracing and both bursting into tears together. Steve and Tom looked aghast at this turn of events and legged it into the garden to escape the emotional scene. Rose did not know quite what to do but did what her mum would have done and switched the kettle on for a brew.

The ladies tried hard to mend their broken friendship over their tea and the men hid in the garden, making themselves busy, regularly checking in on the kitchen to see if it was safe to return. Steve showed Tom the many outbuildings that belonged to Rose. Together they checked the roofs for leaks and damage from the storm. They were pleased that all the outbuildings were as watertight and undamaged as the main house appeared to be.

Val and Doreen appeared to be friends again, but Rose still had some misgivings about Doreen. She was unsure what to make of original The Ship sign and the Captain's paintings that were owned by Doreen. Her recent behaviour towards Rose had been puzzling to say the least. But it was not the time to ask her about the sign or the paintings. To ease her conscience she found herself saying, "Would you like to see the figurehead that we found in the loft? She is a fantastic find and is an integral part of the house. Such a beautiful carving. Come upstairs and I will show you."

She led the way upstairs, past the stained-glass window with the ship from the pub sign depicted. Val followed close behind. Doreen did not look at the window as she passed it. She appeared disinterested in the house itself, but keen to see the infamous figurehead.

The figurehead was gazing across the swollen river and the waterlogged fields beyond. She looked as serene as ever. Doreen rushed to her side and ran her hands up and down her face. "She is so beautiful," she remarked to Rose, "just as you described her." Rose was not listening, she too was gazing, but not at the figurehead or the view, but at the figurehead's hands, her fingers. She was wearing the ring that they had found in the garden earlier. It was not on her right hand though; it was on her left. The figurehead was married. Was she married to the Captain though?

Val was looking at the ring on the figurehead's left hand as well but looked away when Doreen looked across. Rose smiled and thought that Val still had a few misgivings left as well.

But after a moment with the figurehead, Doreen announced, "Thank you so much for letting me see her up close, Rose, but time is getting on and I really must be getting back to the pub."

Rose was amazed that Doreen did not want to stay with the figurehead for long or to look around any other rooms. In fact, she made her excuses and nagged the men for a lift back to the pub shortly afterwards. It was as if the figurehead had rattled her somehow. Doreen's composure was in bits again and she left with watery eyes.

Steve offered to take Doreen back to the pub, but before he left, he asked Rose, "Do you think I could leave working on the Captain's House for a couple of weeks? I have been inundated with calls while you were upstairs. Other villagers who have come a cropper in the storm as well." Rose knew that she was very lucky to have got through the storm without any damage to the Captain's House and if there had been damage, she knew that she would have been right up there at the top of his list. Rose also knew that had Steve not started the Captain's House when he did, the work would have still been outstanding. The Captain's House would have been severely damaged in that storm. The chimney would have surely fallen. Or would it? The house was standing safe in the middle of an island after all that rain. Her Captain's House had sailed safely through the storm.

Forty-Three

Tom stayed with Rose and Mowzer for the rest of the day. They had already fallen into an easy relationship and Rose felt that she had known Tom for years, not just a few days. As the water receded in the village and word got out of the house's miraculous escape from the water, people wandered up the lane to see for themselves. The nosy folk walking up the drive and tramping through the garden. Tom dealt with all this while Rose spent the afternoon reassuring her parents and Lisa that everything was fine with the Captain's House. She even took a call from Greg, the boss from her office who had heard about the flooding and wanted to make sure that she and her new house were fine.

Her mum and dad had not been invited to the house since she had officially moved in, so when they called to check up on her, she invited them to come and see her the following weekend and bring the last of her stuff from her place in town to the Captain's House. Rose was very keen to empty her old London place of her belongings and make a permanent base in Kent in her new house. She was not sure that she wanted to introduce her new man to her parents just yet and was still worried about the fast pace her new love life was taking. She paced up and down the hallway of the house and saw Tom in the kitchen trying not to show that he had been eavesdropping on her conversation with her parents.

Tom grabbed her by the waist as she said her final goodbyes into her mobile phone and pulled her to him with a smile. He kissed her squarely on the lips and looked hard into her eyes. "I noticed you did not mention me, but you spoke about your mysterious Captain and his house. Should I be jealous?" he teased playfully.

Rose returned his kiss with another and gently squeezed his waist before replying, "I did not know how to bring you into the conversation as it has all happened so quickly. You do know that I am not that kind of girl as a rule. I normally take a couple of weeks to even accept a date, it was our first date and we have spent a night together."

Tom and Rose spent the evening in the garden. Tom showed Rose the relics of all the notable roses that she had growing in her garden. All old-style roses. There were no modern hybrid tea roses to be seen in this garden. He took great delight in sharing his horticultural knowledge with Rose. He took her hand and encouraged her to touch the leaves of the roses, feel the texture and stroke the petals of the flowers. He made her sniff the largest blooms, the ones with the most fragrance, and decide which ones she liked best. Rose liked all of them but loved the feeling of his arms and hands guiding her and the sensuous mood of the evening. They worked out that the roses looked like they had been planted in a cottage garden style. There appeared to be a vague hint of a formal rose garden as well. The water had pushed the soil around in the throes of the storm and had revealed pathways that had been hidden. There were just tantalising glimpses of the paths themselves, but none of them led anywhere, which was strange. They explored the garden together until the sun went down. They both made their way back to the house with Mowzer trotting at their feet.

Rose was first into the kitchen and there was a spicy aroma of chicken curry coming from her slow cooker which she had prepared earlier. On closer inspection, there was enough chicken curry in her slow cooker to share. Rose delved in the boxes on the kitchen floor for a couple of bowls and Tom cooked some pilau rice in the microwave. They sat together on the window seat overlooking the river and companionably munched their dinner together. Rose found herself looking at Tom's chest hair sticking out from the top of his T-shirt. The bare flesh of his arms. Looking up at Tom she saw from his expression that she had been rumbled. Her fork crashed into her bowl.

"I was just checking your bowl to see if you had finished and wanted anymore," she said with a hint of smile playing across her lips. Mowzer appeared out of nowhere and leapt into her lap. "Not you, silly!" she cried and gently lowered him to the floor.

"I would love more, but I am not talking about the curry," Tom retorted.

Rose was taken aback by his answer and tried hard not to laugh. The line was so corny, and she could not stifle the laugh in time. She felt that belly-aching laugh erupt and ended up clutching her sides, "Oh that really hurts. That was so awful. You have been watching too many movies. Really. Seriously."

The laugh was infectious, and Tom joined in the laughter until they were both in a tangled heap on the floor, clutching their sides with tears rolling down their cheeks with the effort of trying to stop laughing.

"Ok, so you find my amorous ways funny, so funny. I think I will go home then."

Rose kissed him hard to shut him up. Tom reached up and grabbed her waist and pulled her down on top of him. She did not struggle to get away. She snuggled down and melted into his arms and lost herself in the moment, which seemed to go on forever, until she looked up. A pair of yellow eyes gazed down at hers and she jumped with surprise. Mowzer jumped too. Right into the pair of them. Front paws on Tom and back paws on Rose. Tom took her hand and pulled Rose to her feet and Mowzer tumbled to the floor.

"Sorry, little one," he whispered to Mowzer, "I need your girl." He gently tugged her hand and pulled her upstairs. "It's getting late you know. I better stay the night. You never know, that storm might return. I reckon you would enjoy the company!" he teased.

Rose found herself waking up next to him once again. She smiled at the scene. Mowzer was curled up around Tom's head, using Tom's ears as head and paw rests. Mowzer looked like a furry hat that a child would wear in the winter. They looked so cosy, it seemed a shame to wake them, so she quietly tiptoed out of the bedroom and into the back room to look at the landscape to see if the water had receded further in the night. The fields were still waterlogged but most of the water had drained away. She stood next to the figurehead and leaned her head against hers, mirroring her stance. She looked into the distance and fancied that she could see a figure appearing over the horizon, her Captain returning home after months at sea. The figure continued to walk along the foot path and directly towards the house, Rose dreamily continued watching, eyes feeling heavy and eventually slipping down to sit on the window seat next to the figurehead.

It was here that Tom found her when he awoke. Fast asleep, with her head still facing the sea and the fingers of her left hand curled around the ring that they had discovered in the garden the day before. She looked for all intents and purposes as if she had fallen asleep waiting for someone. Before Tom could wake her, Mowzer leapt on her lap and licked her chin. Rose did not wake as expected and Tom was worried, he took her hand, rubbed it with his, and urged her to wake up. She shrugged his hands away and sighed. Rose was aware that someone was trying to wake her, but she could see her Captain walking towards her and smiling at her. He raised his hand to wave at her, just as Tom had when she first saw him on the footpath. Her dream would not relinquish her. Her anticipation was so great. She had been waiting for so long ...

Tom grabbed her shoulder and turned her away from the window. This was all it took to break the thread of her dream and she woke with a start. She blinked hard at Tom and tried to focus, but part of her was still at the window gazing at her Captain. She blinked again and tried to remember who he was and what he looked like. The Captain or Tom? She could not place either.

Mowzer leapt up at her again. This time drawing blood with his claws in his anxiety to get his mistress back with him once more. This was all it took. Rose was back in the present. She stared in dismay at the blood on her fingers next to the Captain's ring. She stared at Tom uncomprehendingly. It took several minutes before she was herself.

Forty-Four

Tom had to leave early that morning. He was busy for the day, but he only left when he was certain that Rose was back to rights. He was worried about her and did not like to leave her alone. Steve was not due in as he was working elsewhere for a while. James and George were busy helping friends and neighbours with the repairs that were needed in the aftermath of the storm.

Rose had never been fussed over by a man. No man had cared enough to worry about her. Mike had never bothered. Rose had thought that having someone to make a fuss over her would be so romantic, but she had now changed her mind.

The next few days passed quickly. She was busy sorting out the figurehead room into a bedroom for her parents to sleep in. There was just about enough room to put the double bed against a wall without moving the telescope. Rose drew around the telescope with a black marker pen, just in case her mum and dad moved it. She was sure that it was put in that position for a reason. There was no evidence to suggest this, but Rose was certain that it was right there, pointing to a certain spot in the distance. The telescope would need some expert renovation, so it would eventually have to be moved, but Rose was going to cross that bridge when she came to it.

The bedroom overlooking the river was the larger bedroom, technically the 'master bedroom' and when Rose had prepared the room and sat on the bed, she wondered why she had not chosen this room for herself. It did not feel like a bedroom to her. She did not feel as if she could sleep in this room, it was more of a room for waiting.

Rose hoped that her mum would not mind sharing her room with the figurehead. She knew that her dad would be thrilled but she was not sure that her mum would share his sentiments. Rose's dad would probably tell all his mates that he had slept with two women at the Captain's House. She smiled at her dad's antics but made a mental note to ask her mum which room she would be more comfortable sleeping in, as Rose would attempt to sleep in either.

When her mum and dad arrived, Mowzer was playing in the garden, chasing a leaf up and down the garden path. Rose was watching him from the bench and laughing at his game. As the car pulled up the drive it startled the pair of them. Joan had a large bunch of roses for Rose as a housewarming present and her dad was carrying a box of groceries. Neither of them were looking down and did not see Mowzer. They were puzzled as they could not see what Rose was laughing at in the garden. Her dad saw Mowzer at the last minute, just as his boot nearly connected with Mowzer's furry bottom. Both kitten and man howled with surprise.

Rose's mum and dad were pleased to see that Rose had some company at her Captain's House and were equally pleased at the amount of work that had been completed. The house was starting to resemble a home and a cosy one at that. Although there was still some cosmetic work to be done, most of the structural work had been completed. The house was looking good.

Rose's dad, Pete, found the Captain's hat and popped it on his head.

"All you need is your very own Captain now, to keep you company," he said. He replaced the hat on the window seat and chuckled, "Oh, your face was a picture then, sweetheart! Got something to tell us? Has the ghost of the Captain come by to see you?"

Rose was really perturbed by someone trying on her Captain's hat. It unsettled her and made her feel extremely uncomfortable. Her dad sensed this and teased her mercilessly for the next few minutes. Mowzer came to her rescue and curled up in the Captain's hat, looking pretty as a picture when he fell asleep immediately, as only kittens can.

Her mum found the vase that Lisa had bought in her shopping expedition for the house and arranged the roses for Rose. She picked up the vase and took the flowers upstairs. Rose followed her mum and wondered where her mum was going to put the flowers. She had assumed that she would put the flowers on the kitchen windowsill. Joan got to the top of the stairs and was heading for the front bedroom when she caught sight of the figurehead. She stood still and stared. Rose bumped into the back of her and knocked her flying. The flowers and vase flew into the air and the vase smashed into smithereens. Her mum landed heavily in a ungainly heap. Rose managed to stay on her feet.

"What an earth," she cried. "That figurehead looked real for a moment, I swear she turned to look at me," Joan continued. They both looked down at the roses and shattered vase on the floor. The roses were the same as the ones in the figurehead's hands. Big old-fashioned roses.

Forty-Five

The weekend passed without anything else getting broken. Her mum refused to sleep in the figurehead's room, as Rose expected. Joan was delighted with the house and pleased to see Rose looking so happy. Her dad spent the weekend looking around for anything to fix, but all the jobs were either underway or just a bit too complicated for his limited DIY skills. Mowzer was not sure what to make of her dad, due to his near introduction with his boot when they first met. Joan insisted that Mowzer was a darling and spent as much time as Mowzer would tolerate, cuddling him and telling him how very handsome he was.

Rose wondered how she would feel about Tom, as Rose spent most of her time cuddling him as well as Mowzer and dreaming of how handsome he was! She was sure that her mum would think that he was too good to be true and look for some flaws in his character or background. Rose made a mental note to ask Tom if they could visit his brother at his restaurant, so she could find out a bit more about her new man. Although, the more she thought of it the more she reasoned that perhaps she should not ask him but turn up unannounced instead.

Rose found the weekend a huge strain as she wanted her parents to love the house as much as she did. She wanted to impress them and made all their meals in her little kitchen. Her dad found a large wrought-iron table in an outhouse with lots of matching chairs. He cleaned the chairs and table and found space in the corner of the garden. They sat around the new table in the sunshine for their meals. The British summer was glorious. Rose knew that the village was holding its breath for the next weekend to be just as good.

For next weekend was the village fête. Rose had been let off helping this year as she was a new arrival in the village. The ladies of the village had badgered her in the shop to help with one of the stalls, but she stalled for time and instead promised to help next year without fail. The village had started to put up the bunting and coloured flags and Rose had been cajoled into running a length of bunting along her hedge. It looked lovely, flapping merrily in the breeze.

The fete was a traditional one, with the obligatory cake stall, tombola, bric a brac, craft, and other country fare. Doreen and Bob were running the beer tent and Val was in charge of the flower, vegetable, cake, and jam competitions. Rose was asked to enter the flower arranging competition with some of the flowers from her garden. She had declined politely. Her garden overgrown as it was seemed to be full of roses and other cottage plants. There was plenty to choose from for the flower competition, but Rose did not want to enter just yet. She had seen far too many television programmes where everyone had fallen out over the result of a village show. Lots of those had a least one murder or grisly scene. Little did she know that her grisly scene was to be at the village fête, not as gory as she had pictured, but just as dramatic.

The evening that her mum and dad left, Rose had an unexpected visitor. She was sitting out in the garden watching Mowzer playing with scrap of fabric that he had unearthed from the side of the window seat. He was throwing it around, tossing it high into the air and then pouncing on it from as much height as he could muster. Mowzer was leaping and prancing around, making Rose feeling tired just watching him. She was starting to relax and unwind after her mum and dad's visit and was very pleased to have the house to herself once again.

The light was starting to fade, the shadows were getting longer. It was starting to feel a bit chilly, so Rose was debating whether to pop back inside for a jumper or cardigan to put around her shoulders, when she heard a familiar voice coming from the darkening shadows. His blue eyes glinted in the half light and met hers. Mike stepped out from the shadows.

He held a massive bunch of expensive white lilies and reached out to give them to her. She took them from him and then stepped back before he could draw her into one of his passionate kisses. He laughed at her surprise and her unwillingness and gazed beyond her at the house.

"So, this is the infamous Captain's House then, is it?" he questioned. Without waiting for confirmation, he went on, "It is smaller than I expected, but the outbuildings are so unexpected. I have been poking around in them while you were saying farewell to your parents. It would suit me just fine to have an office outside of London and, if you decide not to go back to your job, you can work for me, after we are married."

Rose was speechless. Completely struck dumb by his assumptions and unwitting marriage proposal. She had not heard from him for months, apart from the odd texts and she was unmoved by his apparent sentiments and the fact that he had popped the question, without engaging his brain first. She was furious that he had been poking around her property without even asking her first. She had not searched the buildings properly herself and was perturbed that he had took it upon himself to just wander around. She knew that the utility outhouse was always kept locked, but she was sure that the other buildings had been unlocked when her dad had been putting the extra chairs away for her and making extra room.

Rose held her tongue and looked at the lilies in her hands. She hated lilies, especially white ones. Her mum had always stated that they were something you would take to a funeral. Rose felt a shiver down her spine. They made her think of death.

Forty-Six

Mike did not see the way she looked at the flowers. He did not sense her awkwardness. For he had just returned from a very eventful business trip to the States. He was running on adrenalin and was not expecting any coolness from Rose. He was only ever attentive in person and believed that a short text now and then was all that was needed to keep a woman happy, if he was unable to see them due to business. The money he made, he reckoned, would always be able to make it up to a woman, together with a fancy hotel with all the trimmings and a good time in bed.

For the first time since she moved in, she was not willing to invite someone into the Captain's House. She did not want to share the house with Mike or even show him how much work had been done and how lovely the house was starting to look. She sat back down in the chair and motioned Mike to join her at the table as she lay the lilies on the tabletop. Mike took the hint and sat down, pulling his chair close to hers and readying himself for another attempt at a kiss. Rose did not think that he had missed her that much. She was sure that he would have enjoyed the company of lots of other woman whilst he was away. He was too much of a flirt to stay true to Rose for all that time and she suspected that this was why she had only had a few texts from him as he had felt guilty. Mike was a man of the moment and was easily carried away by his emotions. Rose had loved this about him when she first met him. Back then she could not believe that her boyfriend was so dishy. However, a few months apart had made her see him with all his flaws. Warts and all.

Rose had to sheepishly admit that she was as bad as him, this time. Her dalliance with Tom was at the forefront of her mind and she was scouring the horizon, hoping that Tom would not make a impromptu visit to her that very evening. Rose took a deep breath and started to relay the events of the last few months to Mike. She could see his eyes glazing over and she knew he was not interested in the finer details of the renovation of the Captain's House. She was right, for the first question he asked her when she had finished was, "How much money do you think you could make on it, if you sold it?" She was totally flabbergasted.

"I thought you wanted to use the outbuildings for your offices?" she replied with a smile.

"Oh yes, but I was thinking we could sell the house without the garden and outbuildings and create a small business centre and car park with the rest. A few skips would deal with all the nautical rubbish in the stables and such like. There is nothing of value in there that I can find, I have checked it over for us."

That was all it took for Rose to lose her temper. The royal 'we' was the spark that lit the fire. She stood up and swept the lilies from the table with her hand. She banged the table with her fist and asked Mike in no uncertain terms to leave and never come back. Mike stood up and faced her and grabbed her hands.

He lowered his face to hers and said, "You are my girlfriend, sweetheart, and you mean everything to me." His tone was not loving at all, it was smooth and icy. He glared into her eyes. She met his gaze unwavering, and his blue eyes were cold.

"I was coming to the part where I told you that I had met someone else while you were away. I was trying to break it to you gently as you had clearly missed me. Now I am not sure if you missed me at all, not even a tiny bit. You want my inheritance and everything that goes with it, don't you?" she shouted. It was Mike's turn to get physical and he knocked the chair over completely as he turned to leave.

"I am not finished with you yet, darling," he yelled as he walked away. "I love you far too much," he continued looking back at the Captain's House. "You can tell the guy glaring at me from the bedroom upstairs that it is safe to come down now. I am going."

Rose watched Mike walk away and then raced upstairs to the bedroom. She had not seen Tom arrive and was worried that he had overheard everything. The bedroom was empty when she walked in, there was no one there. Just Mowzer fast asleep on the chair after his exertions in the garden. He was asleep holding the scrap of fabric that he had found earlier. Rose nudged him over a bit with her bottom and sat down and looked back across the garden. Who had Mike just seen in the window? There was no one there and Mowzer would not have been fast asleep if it had been a stranger. Rose was not worried. There was a damp smell coming from the chair. She touched Mowzer's fur to see if it was damp and if he had maybe fallen in the river earlier, but it was bone dry. The smell had a salty tang to it, like the sea. She leant back in the chair and surveyed the room once more. Her back made contact with the sailor's coat that was still hanging on the back of the chair where Rose first found it. It was damp, quite damp, and it smelt of the sea. The makeshift curtains in the window caught a breeze and fanned out across the room, making the smell even more pungent. Her Captain was making his presence known once again.

She reached down and took the scrap of fabric from Mowzer's

paws. The fabric was old and faded, but it was familiar. She had seen it before somewhere in the house. She racked her brains trying to picture where she had seen it before. Then she remembered, it was the same colour as the dress the figurehead was wearing. The exact shade. Faded in the same way. Could the mistress of the house have worn a garment that colour? How uncanny. It seemed there was more than one presence in the Captain's House. His lady was making her presence known too. Mowzer flexed his paws in his dreams, looking for his scrap of cloth. Rose held it tightly and stroked Mowzer gently. She would not be giving him that back to play with. It was too precious.

Forty-Seven

The fine weather continued until the following weekend. Most of the week Rose worried about Mike. He did not call her or pop round to the Captain's House again. She was bemused as to how he found it as she had only given him the address of Little Lanterns and he was never told how near the house was to the Bed and Breakfast. During the end of the week she had popped over to Val's to ask her about Mike and to share her concerns with her motherly friend. She had found Val up to her ears in competition entry forms and found herself roped into helping with the organisation at Val's large kitchen table. Between being told how to process the entries and munching a serious amount of cake, Rose and Val debated how Mike had found her and the Captain's House.

Val reckoned that he would have looked for the nearest village to The Lanterns and Little Lanterns and popped into the local pub to enquire. Rose had to agree that she was probably right as Mike was not some sinister stalker. Just her ex-boyfriend. He had not been to The Lanterns to enquire about her, which Rose had expected. Rose wondered if he was staying in the area, or if he had come down from London on the train, expecting to be asked to stay and make up for the lost time while he was in the States. She wished that she had made time to reply to his texts enquiring about when he could see her again and had replied that she had met someone else. She would not have had to put up with the unpleasantness of his recent visit then.

The only person she had to blame was herself.

Rose had arranged to meet Tom at the fête, Saturday lunchtime. She was excited to meet up with him again. She had chatted with Tom on the telephone in the evenings during the week and had told him of Mike's visit. She expected him to be cross with her for not being totally honest with Mike while he was away. However, Tom was only cross with Mike for looking around the property without asking and presuming that everything was going to be the same after his prolonged absence. Tom did not blame Rose for jumping into bed with him. Of course, he wouldn't! Even if it meant that she had been technically unfaithful. Tom was sure that the reasons relationships failed were because people over thought everything, when people listened to other people and not themselves and their 'inner voice'. He blamed woman for gossiping with each other and winding each other up intentionally. Women's magazines were to blame for it all with their articles on 'good relationships'. Tom reckoned 'chick lit' had a lot to answer for as well.

Rose had worn a summery dress. A cute dress with huge red roses all over the fabric. The dress was her favourite. It made her feel confident and good about herself. She needed the confidence this afternoon and wanted Tom to see her at her best. She began to walk down to the village and met up with David on the way. Val had been at the village green since the crack of dawn getting everything ready and David had done all the morning jobs for the bed and breakfast guests, including cooking the breakfasts. This was normally Val's job and David regaled Rose of the perils of a making a perfect breakfast for his demanding guests as they walked along together. Rose started to worry that Mike had hung about like an unpleasant smell. David assured her that even if he had stuck around, he wouldn't make a scene in front of everyone at a fete, surely! Rose was not so sure. If he met Tom, he might punch him in temper if he saw that he was with Rose. Tom was going to be with Rose all afternoon so the temptation for Mike to start a fight would be huge.

Tom and Rose met outside The Ship and, as they kissed in greeting, they heard a window shut above them. It was just background noise, and they did not look up to see who it was. They made their way to the craft and bric-a-brac stalls and spent time looking at the items for sale. As they wandered around the fete, looking at all the stalls, Tom bought Rose a small, bone china bowl that was hidden at the back of one of the tables. His sharp eyes had spotted a rose. Of course, the bowl was covered in roses. The lady on the stall stated that the rose was one of the most popular designs on bone china. This bowl was small and delicate. It could only be used for very tiny things. Rose was thrilled with her gift and planned to use it for her earrings and other small items of jewellery that she treasured. She looked down at her hand. She had not taken the ring that they had found in the garden, off yet. It fitted perfectly. She had forgotten that it was even there. They met up with Val at the ice cream van. She was red-faced and looked hot and bothered. The stress of the fête was getting to her and she was taking a break with a very large chocolate and mint ice cream. Tom and Rose joined her on the chairs in front of the jazz band with their equally large chocolate ice creams. Rose even had a chocolate flake in hers as well.

They were joined by a large imposing man with a shaggy beard called Stan. He was smartly attired in a suit and waistcoat and was finding the weather was not being kind to his choice of clothing. Rose and Tom were introduced to Stan, who was the main judge of the flower and vegetable competition. He was also the local nurseryman, who owned numerous garden centres in other parts of Kent. He was a jovial man who never relished judging his regular customers but was bribed annually by Val with the free advertising that went in the programme. The free advertising was one of the perks of being a judge. Stan would have preferred to have judged the cooking competitions, but he was not deemed to have the right experience, so the head chef from The Ship dealt with that one. Tom and Stan got on like a house on fire, as they had so much in common. They had met before in a business capacity.

The peace was shattered when a loud yell was heard in the distance. Someone was shouting a name. The shouting got louder as the person got nearer. The name became clearer. "Rose, Rose, Rose. Thought I would find you here, with your new man."

Forty-Eight

There stood Mike, squaring up to Tom, right in front of them all. "I saw you both kissing when I closed my window at the pub earlier. There was no need to flaunt it in front of me, Rose. I expected better from you, sweetheart." Rose shuddered and stepped back, pulling Tom back with her. Tom did not stay at her side, he stepped back up to Mike and offered his hand for a hand shake.

"No hard feelings, mate," he said, "You were in America having fun as well, I bet!" Mike shook his head vehemently from side to side.

"Never, I would never cheat on my Rose." Mike's words sounded hollow and did not ring true. He looked at the floor as he said it and it was obvious that he had played away as well.

The shouting had produced a crowd around them. Right at the front were Steve with his buddies George and James.

Steve made his way to Tom, saying, "You all right there, mate? Is he hassling you? Do you need a hand?"

Rose answered for Tom, "Thank God you are here as well, Steve. Mike is just leaving." Mike looked at Steve who was standing next to Tom, they looked quite daunting as a challenge, standing together. George and James left the crowd and joined them.

"My oh my little Rose petal, sweetheart! How many men have you got through since you have been here?" he taunted. "Anyone else?" he cried.

Then he took the hint and walked away, shaking his head once more from side to side.

Doreen made her way towards them, through the rapidly dispersing crowd. The spectacle was over and the crowd were making their way to the competition marquee as the judging was due to start. Val and Stan left Rose and the men and raced to the marquee. Val had her jobs to do, but before she left she took hold of Rose's arm and told her, "I will be right back after the competitions."

Stan just laughed, "How popular you are, my dear, and you, Tom, are such a lucky man!"

Rose did not know whether to laugh or cry. This was her new home and she had wanted to make a good impression with all the locals and make friends with everyone. Some of the woman caught her eye sympathetically, others were thinking that there was no smoke without fire.

Suddenly Doreen was right there at Rose's side, right there under her nose almost. "Oh, I am so sorry, I did not know Mike knew you, I would never have taken him on as a guest if I had known that there was bad blood between you." Once again, Rose was unsure if she was genuine or just saying the right thing.

Doreen went on to say, "Mike is only staying on for one extra night and he is due to book out on Sunday morning. You will be rid of him then."

Doreen bribed the men back to the beer tent with the offer of a free pint and offered Rose a nice glass of wine.

Rose looked out for Mike as they crossed the village green and saw he was sulking next to the competition marquee well away from the beer tent. He was nursing a pint, but they could steer well clear of him. Steve and Tom noted his whereabouts too. The men stood together, chatting quietly, while keeping their eyes on Mike. Rose stood to one side quietly, pondering how men thought that only women gossiped and then announced that she was going to see what was going on in the marquee.

Tom and Rose then crossed the green, back towards the marquee, and they could hear Val announcing the results over the loudspeaker system. They could hear the excited chatter and then clapping as winners were announced.

"I think I will enter the flower competition next year," she said and was amazed when Tom replied, "Yes, what a wonderful idea, we could enter the competitions together. I am sure there is a vegetable garden hidden amongst all the brambles in your garden."

Rose was overwhelmed by the fact that after such a short while Tom considered that they would be together at the same time next year. She knew they got on very well and she felt that they clicked. Was this man after her Captain's House and all that went with it? she thought and then felt guilty. She blamed Mike for making her think that all men were after her just for her inheritance. She must be going mad, she thought. She had even contemplated that Doreen had ulterior motives as well.

Mike was still standing on the periphery of the village green. He was looking rather worse for wear and still looked angry. He noticed the pair of them and glared daggers at them both.

The marquee was crowded and hot, but Rose wanted to see what had won, in order to get some ideas for next year. The flowers had to be arranged to a certain specification and there was a special class for roses. Just one stem with one single flower. All the exhibits were of the modern hybrid rose type. There were no old roses in the rose class, just the usual hybrid tea roses, the ones you would find in the supermarket aisles and standard garden centres. Tom and Rose exchanged knowing glances. That would change next year for sure.

Forty-Nine

It was early evening when Rose made her way back to the Captain's House to check on Mowzer and give him his supper. Tom was giving her a lift back in the van. Rose enjoyed riding in the van as it was slightly higher than her car and she could see over the hedgerows and walls on the way back. She enjoyed being nosy and looking at everything she did not normally see. As they rounded the bend in the road and drew level with her hedge, she noticed that the doors were open in her stable block. She pointed it out to Tom who slowed down and peered across her. He drew to a halt just before her gate and said, "You should stay put and I will check it out."

Rose agreed but regretted her choice as he disappeared into the garden. She couldn't see the outbuilding from this vantage point so would not be able to see what was going on. She was getting concerned for Tom's safety. She left the van and crept into the garden, being as quiet as she could. She could hear Tom before she could see him, talking with another man. She could not identify the other man's voice. She then saw Christian standing beside Tom, trying desperately to explain that Rose knew who he was, and it was all right. Tom groaned when he caught sight of her.

"I thought I told you to stay in the car," he said.

"Good job I didn't. He is more than welcome on my property. His name is Christian." She turned to face Christian and continued, "I have not seen you around for a while. Is everything OK?"

Christian explained, "I have been offered an old boat to live in. It's on at the shingle beach at the moment as it is not seaworthy. It is the perfect home for me. There is not much room, but enough room for all my stuff. I have come back to the Captain's House to collect the rest. The boat is very old and needs a lot of work, so I will be staying put for a while. I guess I can put that right over the rest of the summer and the winter months. I plan to relaunch her next spring."

Rose was pleased that everything was coming together for Christian. She was not sure how she would have felt about him kipping in the outhouses or the stables while she was all cosy and warm in the house during the winter. She knew it was his choice, but she was sure she would have ended up offering him a room for the winter and gained a lodger unintentionally. Christian was pleased that he had caught Rose.

"I am worried that things have been moved around and disturbed in your outbuildings. I am not sure that anything is missing but it could well be."

Rose immediately thought of Mike and she took a look at Tom's face and she was sure that he was thinking the very same thing.

"I know that the garden table and chairs have been moved, but can I check everything else just in case? I am sure I could tell if something is out of place," Christian said.

They checked all the buildings, and they could all see that things had been moved. The dust was disturbed in places and the tarpaulin and covers over all the stored items had been messed up. The covers had not been put back straight, so it was obvious.

"You know there are valuable bits and pieces in the Captain's store, Rose?" Christian said.

"You said that everything was junk, when we talked about this before, I am sure you did? That is why I have not been out here yet. I was concentrating on the main house first."

Christian was adamant, "I would not have been that flippant to you, Rose! I was stressed when I met you, I hate change." Christian led Rose into a large building. "This is where the captains kept all their stuff and that," he went on. "This is the Captain's store, I reckon."

The place was piled high with furniture and boating paraphernalia.

Christian took one look and announced, "The paintings have been moved. They were always on that side of the building. Someone has been looking at them."

At this point, Rose did not even know that there were ever any paintings in the building. She was sure that if her dad had found anything like that when he was exploring, he would have let her know. She guessed that it was Mike that had found them and looked at them. To think that Mike had said that there was nothing of any value!

Tom, Rose, and Christian lifted the coverings and looked at the paintings one by one. They were remarkable. The paintings were colourful and mostly of the sea with ships and harbours. Right at the back there was a painting of a garden. The very same painting that was in the pub. It was identical, but which one was the original? Mickey had said that the Captain had painted the painting in the pub in lieu of his bar bill. Had he copied this one, she mused?

Tom peered at the paintings, "I haven't a clue about paintings, but I am sure that if I had a bar bill to pay, and I could paint, I would copy the original and give the copy away to the landlord."

Fifty

Rose was having a restless night after the events of the day. Her mind was having trouble processing all the surprises of the day. Why has Mike turned up again, like the proverbial bad penny? Christian and Tom had brought the paintings inside the house and stacked them in the back bedroom next to the figurehead. Tom had sensed Rose's turmoil and left her alone to sort it out. Now Rose wished she had begged him to stay. In the morning, she would need someone to hold her close and help her work out what to do. Mowzer was doing his best to cuddle her, and she found his purr once again a comfort, but the day had disturbed her. It was now stopping her from sleeping. What was on her mind and worrying her most of all was Tom. Tom had appeared in her life the perfect, mysterious stranger in her life and her bed. Everything was perfect, but was Tom, really? Tom was spending a lot of time in her house and garden. It was Tom who found the ring, but was Tom just mirroring her surprise in the outbuildings or had he already found the paintings? Was he as perfect as he seemed? Would she be better off spending her time with Steve, she knew without a doubt that she could trust him? Rose tossed and turned all night and ended up pacing the floor next to the paintings. In the end, she sat down next to the figurehead, exhausted. A warmth radiated from the figurehead into Rose. Rose's head rested next to her dress and as the floor started to sway, she was lulled into a deep, dreamless sleep.

In the morning, she decided that she would take the paintings over to Lisa and then onto Lisa's parents' business premises and ask them to look at them for her. She was sure that she held the originals but wanted to find out more. Would she find out more about her elusive Captain if it turned out that he was the painter? Rose was in the kitchen making her first cup of the day. She was staring out of the window, into the distance, trying to figure it all out. She heard a tap on the back door, which was wide open. Mowzer was prowling in the doorway, pretending to stalk an imaginary mouse. Her uninvited visitor stepped over the kitten and made her way into the kitchen.

There, right in front of her, was Doreen. Rose nearly dropped her mug in surprise. This was the last person she had expected to visit. Rose tried to hide her surprise and turned away to fill the kettle with more water for her guest. Doreen announced in a whisper that she had to tell Rose something.

"Your Mike has just told me that there are paintings in your outbuildings!"

Intrigued, Rose urged Doreen to go on.

"Mike ate his breakfast at the table next to the painting of the Captain's garden just a couple of hours ago. Mike made a sarcastic comment to me about how nice the painting was. He then said, 'I have seen that painting before at that old house that belongs to Rose, in one of the outbuildings.' Is that true, you have found some paintings here?"

"I only found the paintings yesterday and don't know what to do about them yet," Rose admitted, sheepishly. "I have had a sleepless night worrying about it all."

"I am not surprised you cannot sleep in this house, but I have had more sleepless nights than you, worrying about my paintings. I guessed that the originals were up here in this spooky house somewhere," Doreen whined.

Rose had a hunch that Doreen had already had the paintings in the pub valued. She was right. They were copies and therefore almost worthless. This meant that Rose held the original paintings. They could be worth a fortune. Doreen explained with a sigh that she was sure that the pub's paintings were the only way out of their financial difficulties. The pub sign, it turned out, was not worth that much either.

Doreen said, "Mike offered to come back here and swap the paintings over before you even knew they were there. He wanted a share in the profit though!"

"You have got to be joking, Mike offered to do that?" Rose could feel her voice getting louder and her temper rising. She could well believe this though, as Mike was more motivated by money than anything else. She did not have him down as dishonest, but there was a first time for everything. It looked like she had a very lucky escape from him.

"I don't mean you any harm. I am not going to swindle you. I know you must think I am dodgy now. I am desperate to find some money from somewhere, but not that desperate to steal from you."

Rose could not dispel her concerns about Doreen, but it sounded like she was telling the truth and it was all starting to add up. It explained Doreen's behavior in the pub and more recently when she had visited the house after the storm. Rose fought against all her good manners and did not offer her the obligatory cup of morning coffee even though the kettle had now boiled.

"I have an appointment this morning, so I really have to get ready now," Rose stated with more confidence than she felt. Doreen stood up to leave and impulsively hugged Rose goodbye as she left.

Rose's composure shattered when Doreen finally left her alone.

She felt her bottom lip tremble and she needed to sit down.

As her appointment was fictitious, Rose took her time getting washed and dressed. She wanted some time to herself. She tried not to look in the bathroom mirror at the reflection of the figurehead. She avoided everything connected with the Captain, as she did not want to be rattled any further. She planned to move the paintings somewhere else, for safekeeping prior to getting them valued. There was far too much speculation about how much they were worth by everyone, except her. She did not have them insured or anything. She was not going to be silly enough to leave them in the house when everyone she had talked to in the last 24 hours seemed to have an opinion on them.

Rose made a quick call to Val to ask her if she had somewhere secure for her to store the paintings. She then called Steve as she knew he was working in the village, to see if he would help her move the paintings if he had some time during the day. Her friends were only too pleased to help. Steve was keen to look at the paintings.

He turned up with his ready smile and said, "Look at you, what have you found now? This house is turning out to be full of surprises!"

Rose was pleased to see Steve. His sunny nature and smiles were infectious. They both filled the van with paintings, which did not take as long as expected. Some were just canvases; others were encased in heavy ornate frames. The framed paintings did not match the Captain's House rustic style. Rose and Steve wondered where they would have been hung, it would have had to be quite a grand house to match the impressive frames.

Val was sitting in the garden when they arrived at The Lanterns, waiting for Steve and Rose.

"Another lady waiting for me in her garden, this afternoon," Steve joked. "If I wait until mid-afternoon, perhaps they will become scantily dressed as the day is warming up nicely!"

David came out to lend a hand as well. In no time at all, the paintings were safely stored and locked away under the stairs in The Lanterns. Val's ironing board, Hoover, and other cleaning stuff were now in the middle of the hallway. David was told to put them away in his study for now. Val wanted to keep the paintings locked away for Rose. This cupboard under the stairs had plenty of security, including two hefty modern locks. The cupboard contained their small household safe. The paintings just fitted in, but several of the larger ones in frames would have to be stored in their loft instead.

Rose planned to take them to Lisa's parents as soon as she could, but in the meantime, they were not in the house and somewhere no one would think of looking.

Fifty-One

Rose had found the dusty old book when she first looked at the house and had slipped it into her pocket and forgotten all about it. When she came across it again, she put it to one side on her bedside table. It had sat there most of the summer, ignored and forgotten, as Tom was keeping her company. She had no need for any book.

It was what was known as an 'Indian summer'. The nights were long and very hot. Rose had spent most of the long, hot nights with Tom. The man she had met and fell head over heels in love with midsummer. Rose could not believe her recent good fortune and inheritance which had resulted in her owning this fabulous house. There was still lots of work to be done in the house and the garden. On the odd nights that Tom was not there, Rose had once again sensed the Captain. Sometimes she saw a faint outline of a person in the shadows, or she heard distant footsteps on the paths in the garden.

Rose was on her own tonight though, tossing and turning in the covers, desperately seeking sleep in the warm night. Her arm stretched out to match her leg that was sticking out of the covers to get cool and knocked the book off the cabinet, making an almighty clatter and waking Rose out of her slumber. She switched on the lamp and examined the book.

The book was leather backed, dusty, and very smelly. It felt slightly damp, although this was impossible after the heat of the last couple of weeks. It smelt like most things in the house, salty and 'of the sea'. It was filled with ineligible writing. Soft, flowing text, very curly, neat, and impossibly small. Rose peered at the words again and again, and turned each of the pages, looking for something, anything that she could decipher. About half of the way through the book, there was a diagram. It looked familiar, very similar to the shape of the front garden and the plot of land that surrounded the house. The house was not shown within the plot, just the land with some peculiar symbols and shapes. The river was clearly marked, as was the beach and the ocean beyond. Rose went back to the beginning of the book and tried in vain to pick out some words in the illegible text. She lay back and snuggled back down into the pillows to get comfortable and raised the book up towards the lamp as if the extra light would make any difference. It didn't so she turned onto her side and peered again, feeling sleepy. Within moments, Rose was fast asleep clutching the book to her chest, like a child holding her teddy and more recently like she held Tom during the night time hours. Mowzer, her black and white tom cat, crept into the bed beside her and laid his head on the book, purring contently and looking across at the chair, which contained a faint shadow gently shimmering in the semi-darkness.

The garden at the Captain's House had gone berserk in the bright, almost tropical sunshine that had shone almost daily. There were flowers everywhere. Big, blossoming roses swaying and nodding in the breeze and tiny delicate daises smothering the grass with their flowers. The cottage garden almost hid the house from sight, the flowers and greenery almost reaching the top of the ground floor windows. The river that ran almost alongside the property was still flowing freely, as, although it was hot, there were a fair few showery days and downpours that accompanied the thunderstorms. The river bubbled across the pebbles in the shallows, but the deeper parts of the river were fast and furious. The fast-flowing water, a constant reminder of the flood that nearly engulfed the house earlier in the summer.

The water could be heard in the bedroom, just a little bubble at first, then the steady hum of the fast-flowing river. Then, that turned into the sound of the waves crashing into the shingle on the shore and then at last the gentle wash of waves against the wooden hull of a boat, floating just floating …

The figure in the armchair faded into the shadows once more and the room was empty, but for the sound of the waves and the salty tang of the sea in the air. As the dim dawn light crept into the house, she started to stir. Mowzer was right there in Rose's face. Ready to face the day and impatient for his breakfast. A decisive paw swiped Rose across the cheek, not once but twice. Then, on getting no response from the sleepy Rose, Mowzer went in for the attack and swiped just once more with his claw slightly extended. She gasped and sat up straight and knocked Mowzer and the book on the floor. The book glanced Mowzer a sidewards blow as they tumbled through the air together.

Mowzer was forgotten as, she reached out and picked up the book from the floor and gazed at the dusty cover. Lost in thought she leant back into the pillows, just as she had during the night, and started to flick through the pages once again. Oblivious to the cries of the indignant cat, she settled down with the book, sniffing the air and sighing as she once again could smell the ocean.

The book was still illegible in the cold light of day, but the book opened once more onto the pages which contained the plan of the land, her land, but without the house … Where was the house and why would the author show the exact boundaries of the property without showing the house? There was always a mystery with her house, she thought. The book, the carvings, the hidden figurehead had all been uncovered, but what was the connection and why was Rose so drawn to the house?

Meanwhile, Mowzer sat at the side of the bed, ignored by his mistress and crying loudly for his breakfast.

Fifty-Two

Rose's mobile phone made her jump, chirping loudly to announce a text message it continued to chirp for several minutes, as text after text arrived. It seemed that the world was trying to get her attention. She sat up in bed, snatched her phone out of her open handbag on the floor, and peered at the screen. The date was shown on the left-hand side of the screen and could be seen in bold type over her wallpaper of Mowzer looking very cute curled up his Captain's hat. The date taunted Rose as she was sure it was important. A glance at her messages and the list of senders gave her a big clue. It was the date of her return to work in London and she had managed to oversleep and sit around reading, instead of making sure she caught the train into London and back to the office.

The messages were from Tom, her mum and dad, and best friend Lisa. They were all wishing her well and trying to second guess what her decision would be. Over the spring and summer months, Rose had taken some unpaid leave from the office and was obliged to return to negotiate the terms of her old position or resignation. She was still not sure what to do, her friends thought that she was hiding the information and was going to announce her decision with a flourish in the local pub that evening. The decision was still unmade and as she went about getting washed and dressed in her formal office clothes, she tossed the reasons around in her head.

She did not need to go back to the office right now and commute into town, but it was the only job she had known since leaving college and she was good at what she did. Most days she enjoyed it, but some of the characters in the office were challenging and she had enjoyed being away from the office politics. She had some money left over from her recent inheritance and had almost finished the house but had not yet made a start on the outbuildings. The outbuildings could have lots of uses and she was sure she could use them to make money. She could rent them out as business spaces or make them into another property to use as a let or self-catering holiday property, like her neighbour and good friend Val. Val had no shortage of guests and often had to turn people away as she was full. Val was not keen on dogs, so would not let any of her accommodation to anyone with a dog, but Rose loved any kind of animal, as long as they were well behaved. Several of the local businessmen, including Steve, the builder who worked on the Captain's House and was about to give Rose a quote on the renovation of the outbuildings, needed space to use as office and storage space. She could run their admin stuff all from the comfort of her own home.

As she parked in the tiny car park at the station and paid a ridiculous price for her return ticket to London, she continued to fret about what to do. The train was packed. She had to stand for part of the way. Everyone was engrossed in their books, phones, and tablets and no one was interested in the beautiful scenery that they were passing or each other. It was a while since Rose had travelled this way and she marveled at how insular everyone was. How boring it all was and how she would hate to have to do the journey every day. She then contemplated working part time in London and only having to travel maybe a couple of days every week. A little extra money, just in case something went wrong with her new plans. It could be the ideal compromise.

The crushing atmosphere on the tube and the overpowering smell of sweaty bodies that greeted her swiftly admonished her of that notion. Full time or part time, Rose had no intention of doing either. Her mind was made up, it was probably made up months ago, when she walked out of the office and had started her unpaid leave, but she had to think through all the alternatives as the last thing she wanted was to lose her beloved Captain's House because she had run out of money and had given up a perfectly good job on a whim or for the benefit of her ghostly Captain.

Tom had been very good at letting her make her own mind up, but she still worried that he was only dating her because he wanted to get his hands on the Captain's House and the rare shrub roses that were growing in the garden. It was clear that Tom adored Rose, but he deliberately avoided any discussion on the future of the house and what Rose would do for a job. Just the once, in an unguarded conversation, one morning, Tom had said that he had always imagined the house as an upmarket hotel, with an extra wing to accommodate more guests. A restaurant within for his brother and extensive gardens and greenhouses for his roses. He did not mention this again, Rose did not know any of the finer details of his ideas as he kept them to himself. If she asked him, she was sure that he would tell her. Or would he?

Fifty-Three

It has been a difficult day and Rose was absolutely shattered when she got back to the house that evening. Mowzer was waiting for her on the doorstep and his displeasure in her first long absence from him was patently obvious. His welcome was frosty. His head and tail were held aloft as he paced up and down by the door. Rose fumbled with the door and had trouble fitting the key into the lock.

Rose was hot, sticky, and very bothered. The events of the day had unnerved her and although she was sure that she had made the right decision, there was a panicky feeling in the pit of her stomach that was making her feel physically sick. As she fed the impatient Mowzer, the smell of the cat food assailed her nostrils and made her tummy inwardly heave. As she stood up to stand from her crouching position over Mowzer's food bowl, she felt dizzy and grabbed the work top for support. She had hoped that when she returned home she would feel better but that was not the case. She felt worse, so much worse, so she took herself up to bed.

The bedroom was looking worse for wear as she had left it in a hurry that morning, but she just kicked off her high-heeled work shoes and crept under the covers. It was another warm night, but she was not in a mood to care. She pulled the duvet up over her head and wished that reality would go away. She was scared, so scared that she had made the wrong decision. She had ditched her job, handed in her resignation, and was going to go with her heart. Do something with her inheritance, the land, and the house to support herself. She had a limited amount of money and as much time as she wanted, but the thought of failing and losing the lot was more than she could cope with.

The decision that had felt so right was now real and she had to 'step up to the plate', as Lisa, her best friend, would say. She got hotter and hotter under the duvet with her mind racing away from her, until Mowzer pounced on her inert shape on the bed and made her surface again. He settled on her chest and looked up at her face with big, wide eyes. She found herself smiling at her furry friend and cuddled him tight, making him purr with delight.

She sat there for a while, until she started to regain her composure and her stomach stopped churning around and around like a malfunctioning washing machine. Her and Mowzer against the world, she thought. Her thoughts started to settle as her equilibrium settled. She had all her new friends and Tom of course. Everyone would be on her side. She was not sure that The Ship was going to be the best place to celebrate not going back to work. Doreen was trying hard to make amends for her somewhat less than warm welcome, back in the summer. Doreen had rekindled her friendship with Val, but Rose was still a little uncertain of Doreen and felt that she was not entirely honest.

Rose decided that she would not tell everyone her plans for the future of her Captain's House in the pub this evening. She did not want Doreen to think that she would steal some of her business if she decided to turn the outbuildings into self-catering properties or run a Bed and Breakfast establishment. Val, she was sure, would be supportive and would probably send her excess customers to her, without question. Rose wanted to get it all sorted in her own head first and did not want to antagonise Doreen unnecessarily. Tom was supportive of whatever decision she made, but she had not talked it out with him. She could not shake her original misguided opinion completely that he was only dating her for the house. He had given her no reason to think otherwise, but from time to time he seemed to disappear into the garden, quietly poking at the dirt and muttering to himself, as if he were looking for something.

Rose and Mowzer cuddled together until a creaking noise startled them from their slumber and dreaming. Mowzer heard it first and twitched his ear and turned his head to track the sound. His sudden movement alerted Rose. She knew that they were the only ones there. She watched Mowzer with a frown and her heart started to race. Mowzer continued to sit still, just listening. His body was relaxed, but he had stopped purring. As they listened together, Rose absently started to stroke the cat's body, her fingers gently moving across his velvety fur. The creaking sound seemed to be coming from the floorboard's downstairs, the sound of someone walking about. There was a heaviness to the tread.

Rose could not sit still any longer and lifted Mowzer gently from her and settled him on the floor. As she stood up her head felt heavy, and the room started to spin. Her vision became blurry, and her arms started to feel as heavy as her head. The heaviness descended slowly to her feet. She was unable to move a muscle and her head swam. Mowzer scampered away from her, his claws clinking on the wooden floorboards as he moved. Rose heard him gallop down the stairs and stop suddenly as if he had collided with something or someone at the bottom of the stairs. Then there was a surreal hush, a quietness that filled the house.

She stared at her feet through the haze that had accompanied the heaviness and willed them to move. Then, there was no sound at all. Nothing.

Fifty-Four

It seemed like an age until Rose was able to move. While she was still, every other sense was on high alert and she could feel the air swirling around her. Taste the air, even. A dusty, salty taste settled on her tongue. A strange salty tang reached her nostrils. Her ears strained to hear Mowzer.

She fell forward suddenly as her body started to move. Her brain had finally sent the messages to her body. It was as if she was a clockwork toy and the mechanism had stopped. When it restarted, everything happened at once. She put out her hands to save herself and landed in a heap on the floor.

She got up and ran to the top of the stairs, looking down she saw Mowzer. He was winding himself silently around an empty space, rubbing his face against … nothing. There was nothing there. Mowzer was making no noise, his paws, claws, and body silent on the wooden floor. So very silent.

He stopped and looked up the stairs at Rose. His eyes were wide and filled his little furry face, they seemed to twinkle and glisten in the coloured light from the stained-glass window in the landing. His body was bathed in a multi-coloured sheen from the window too. Rose shook her head and tried to reconcile what she had just seen with reality. She knew what it looked like and what she wanted to believe. Mowzer and the Captain. Her Captain.

Rose sighed and sat on the top stair. Her legs still felt wobbly, and her head ached. She gazed down the stairs at Mowzer who had sat down and was washing himself without a care in the world. He had not rushed up to comfort her and she was ever so slightly jealous! She carefully paced downstairs and into the kitchen to take her mobile phone out of her handbag on the work surface. She dialed Tom first. There was no answer and she was straight through to his voicemail. It was only then that she looked at the time on her phone and realised that Tom was on his way. Several hours had passed since her return from London and she had missed her chance to cancel. She raced upstairs, taking the stairs two at a time.

When Tom knocked at the door a little while later, she was almost ready and putting her lipstick on in the bathroom mirror. She could barely make out her face, let alone her lips in the steam. Her bathroom was hot and steamy after her rushed bath and hair wash. She drew a smiley face with her index finger and mirrored the smile with her own.

She opened the door to Tom and peered around the edge.

"Only me," said Tom with a grin, "why the caution, who were you expecting instead of me?"

"Just you," she replied, answering his grin with one of her own. "So nice to see you after the day I have had. Crazy, so crazy. Just like my headache, it is wearing off a bit, but please don't shout."

"Oh yeah, why should I shout at you? What have you done?"

"You haven't even waited until you were inside the house, have you?" she joked. "I will tell you with the others, when we get to the pub, you will have to wait ..."

The bar was crowded, but there was a subdued atmosphere in The Ship when Tom and Rose arrived. Val was standing at the bar, she gave Rose a warning glance and told them both to sit with the others and she would bring the drinks over.

Rose and Tom joined their friends at the table. Val returned laden with drinks and sat down at the table, drawing the chair out so that she had her back to the bar.

"They have decided to sell up and cut their losses, you know," Val whispered across the table.

Rose was taken aback by this news. "Seriously, you can't mean that? I thought that business was picking up. Weren't you sending your extra guests to the pub?"

"Yes, we still are. I think we were just a little too late to help turn the business around for them. What a shame. I wonder what will happen to this place and who will buy it now?"

Rose looked around at her friends and could see that they were all thinking the same thing. Another traditional country pub turned into swanky apartments or turned into a second home for a wealthy businessman who had no interest in the area or the local people.

"Don't suppose you have any spare cash left over?" Steve asked Rose. "Or could your new business plans include The Ship with a little messing about" Rose knew that Steve was fishing for information. Information about her plans for her future. He had got up and was gently nudging her with his shoulder to emphasize his point. Her friends all looked at her intently and waited for her answer. Rose did not want to give too much away, especially at such a difficult time for Doreen.

"I have resigned from my London job, with some ideas for the future. More details to follow," she teased her friends. She was so glad she had not embellished her plans, as just then she caught a glimpse of Doreen out of the corner of her eye making her way to join the others at the table. Rose stood up and embraced Doreen with a heartfelt hug. How awful, to have all your dreams dashed. Her own nightmare, when she was hiding from the world under the covers earlier. That nightmare had come true for Doreen. She needed to ensure that whatever she did worked for her. That it made money and not a loss. As she looked around at the table, she knew that if she included her friends then between them they could make it work. Poor Doreen, she made her friends too late in the day and was set to lose her business and dream. It was a sobering thought for Rose.

Fifty-Five

Rose spent the evening sandwiched between Steve and Tom. Her every need was answered. Steve bought her dinner and Tom kept her thirst at bay by buying her drinks and then tempting her with a chocolate dessert. He whispered into her ear, "I have another dessert for you when we get back to the house." As she turned to look at him and give him an equally saucy retort, she caught sight of Steve, grimacing and pulling a face at her. She was pleased that Steve was happy for her as she knew he liked her too. Rose had never had one guy that into her, let alone two guys that were interested at the same time. She knew that Steve was playing it cool. Looking after her from a distance and willing her to get fed up with the passion with Tom or for Tom to make a mistake.

Tom caught the look from Steve as well. He gave him a 'hard luck' face and then urged Rose to call it a night.

"You said you had a headache back at the house before we left. We should be making tracks."

"That will dash your plans then, mate," Steve replied with a smile.

"Yeah, I guess, but you looked a little green round the gills, sweetie, when I arrived. There was a peculiar smell in the house too."

"I have some time tomorrow," said Steve, "I will check over that boiler for you, just to make sure. You hear some horror stories about boilers and stuff. We need to make sure you are alright."

Val looked up. "Rose, you look a little sheepish, did you have another spooky moment with your infamous Captain?"

"Of course not, Val, the house makes noises all the time, I just need to get used to them."

It was not the first time that Rose had not confided in her friends and Tom. She was sure that everyone would insist in her not staying in the house or suggesting that Tom moved in with her. She loved her new home and did not want to share it with anyone but Mowzer at the moment.

The house had turned her into a bit of a recluse of late. Val and Tom said that she was turning into her great aunt, who had been well loved in the village, but famous for not going out and getting everyone to deliver her shopping. She was generous and made large donations to every local fund-raising event, but never attended in person. As she grew older, the younger generation used to think she wasn't real. It was said that she never left the village in her lifetime, never went abroad or even to London. Luckily, she was in good health till the day she died. So, she left the house, feet first, to the village undertaker and church, which was her last wish.

Her great aunt had always stated that she would never get lonely in her house as there was plenty of company. She was often to be seen wandering around her rose garden talking to herself. Or was she? Rose had an idea that she was talking to the Captain. Tom had shared a childhood memory of watching her great aunt chattering away on the garden bench. He was playing in the garden while his family were on the beach, hiding behind a large shrub rose. She had startled him as he was sure that she was talking to him. He hid behind the bush until she had wandered away to put the kettle on for tea, growing stiff and being too scared to move in case she caught him in her garden and forbade him from coming again.

Tom had loved the garden from when he first saw it, aged about seven. He was fond of saying that that garden was the seed from which his love of gardening had grown.

When Tom and Rose arrived back at the house that evening, it was dark. Rose had left lamps on in the windows which glowed brightly in the darkness and cast a welcoming light on the paths leading up to the house. It was the first time that Rose had done this, and she was delighted at the effect. Tom enveloped her in a big hug on the doorstep and pulled her close to him. He held her tightly and she lifted her head to his, as she knew he was leaning down to kiss her. Their lips met, and they shared a passionate kiss. It all felt just too perfect, and Rose pulled away from him, suddenly unsure. Where this feeling came from, she did not know, but she knew she did not want him staying over. With an unsteady smile, she slid out of his arms and slipped inside the house. Tom was left on the doorstep once again, just like he was when he picked her up earlier.

"Oh Rose, is everything OK?"

"I really don't know, but I have had a busy, busy day and the headache has just returned with a vengeance so perhaps we should leave it there for tonight."

"Really, after all your promises tonight? You sure I can't change your mind … All right then, I will call you first thing in the morning to make sure you are really OK."

He walked off down the path to his van, looking back every couple of paces. Rose stood still in the doorway, wondering why she had a compelling urge to have the house to herself and why she had turned him away.

She stepped back into the hallway and closed the door. She leaned against it and slid down the door to the floor, it was then she noticed

Mowzer in front of her, once again winding his little body round and round an empty space. There was still nothing there.

Fifty-Six

True to his word, Tom phoned at first light the next day. The phone startled Rose and Mowzer, who were curled up together in a tight ball. Rose knocked Mowzer off the bed for the second morning in a row and with a loud squeal he left the bedroom, too indignant to even ask for his breakfast.

Rose swiped the screen of her mobile and listened to the rich tone of Tom's voice, stretching every limb as she did so. "Rose, I was wondering how you are this morning and if I could pop over soon? Do you want to discuss your ideas with me, now you have made your mind up?"

"My goodness, you have just woken me, not sure which way is up right now. You can pop over whenever you like. I think the headache has gone, but I am so tired."

"Tell you what, I will let you sleep in for a bit and then come over. I'll call into the shop for some pastries and a newspaper. See you soon."

With that he was gone. Rose was left holding her mobile in her hand with no connection. Tom was so sure that Rose would want to see him, he had not even waited for an answer. Rose hated anyone making decisions for her which was the reason why she had left home. Her mum and dad, like most parents, had tried to run her life and make all the important decisions long after they needed to. Her mum was her best friend and loved to chat but insisted on her point of view.

Her dad just pointed out the pitfalls in everything. They had not budged when she had asked their advice on the house. Her mum wanted her to share the house with someone. A lodger or an eligible man, to share the bills and be safe. Her dad just frightened her with potential building regulations and financial restraints. She was pleased that her parents wanted to talk through her life, even though it was annoying. It meant they cared and loved her. She wouldn't change them for the world.

After her busy day yesterday, she was too tired to think about it all and turned over and went back to sleep.

Tom woke her for a second time. The weather was turning and the heat of the end of summer was subsiding. There was a dampness to the air and an autumnal chill. Rose climbed out of bed, shivered, and went to close the window that she had left wide all night. She cursed herself for not closing it and peered over the ledge and down into the garden at Tom. True to form, he was kicking the dirt around with his feet, while waiting for her to open the front door.

"You are making a mess with the dirt again, you," she called to him.

"Oh yeah, you never know what you might find in the dirt here," he teased and winked at her.

"I will be straight down and will have to let you in before you make too much of a mess."

Rose opened the door and pulled at the sleeves of her long-sleeved T-shirt that she used as a nightshirt. The chill of the air was not what she was used to, so she was not amused when Tom grabbed her arm and pulled her to the edge of the path, right to where he had kicked the dirt all over the place.

"Look right there, the path continues into the lawn, or should I say grass, there is no way your front grass can be described as a lawn just yet!"

Rose rubbed her eyes and pulled her arm back to her side, giving Tom a playful nudge as she did so.

"You continue playing in the dirt and I will warm those pastries in the microwave, stick the kettle on and get dressed. It's not warm enough to play in the dirt this morning with you and I have my knickers and legs on full view."

"The view is just fine with me, but I would welcome some lunch, it's too late for breakfast now!"

Rose glanced down at his watch and noted that it was half past one in the afternoon. She had slept through the morning and into the afternoon.

"How come I slept through that late? Where is Mowzer, he has not had his breakfast? Mowzer? Mowzer?"

Mowzer did not appear as he normally did when she called him. Particularly when he had an empty belly. Rose called him over and over again. Where was her handsome boy? Why was he not answering her calls? She pictured Mowzer winding his little body round the empty space last night and wondered if he was up to something with the Captain.

Fifty-Seven

Rose popped the kettle on and, while it was boiling, rushed upstairs. She nipped into the bathroom and had a quick wash and then dashed into the bedroom and threw on some jeans and a fresh T-shirt, after quickly squirting some deodorant under her arms. She may have had a lie in and ditched her job, but she was not going to let her standards slip. She looked around the room as she got ready, glancing in all Mowzer's favourite places in case he was curled up asleep and intentionally ignoring her and his rumbling belly.

The bedroom was empty. She had fastened the window before she went downstairs to greet Tom, but as she gazed out, a little face peered in. Mowzer was outside on the windowsill and waiting for her to let him in. He was not prepared to jump down and had been waiting patiently for her to let him in. She immediately felt foolish for thinking that he was with the Captain and was pleased that she had not voiced her thoughts out loud to Tom. What he had been doing on the windowsill in the first place was still a mystery, but he was safe, or he would be when she let him back in.

As she walked to the window, Mowzer stood up and proceeded to walk up and down the sill, weaving from side to side. Several times it looked like he was going to fall off. Although it is a well-known fact that cats always land on their feet, Rose was not sure that her Mowzer could do so. She need not have worried for as she opened the window and he deftly jumped back into the room, right below her was Tom, his arms outstretched ready to catch Mowzer in case he fell.

"That was a close call. I must have shut him out when I closed the window when you arrived. You would have thought he would have made a noise when I was calling him earlier. Do you think he was sunbathing on the sill when I shut it?"

"Can't say I noticed, Rose. I would think he would have made his presence known when you were closing the window! Shall I make the tea, I think I heard the kettle boil?"

"Oh yeah, I was making some tea. Completely forgot, what with Mowzer messing about. Yeah, you make the tea and I will warm the pastries."

Mowzer trotted down the stairs in front of her as if nothing had gone on and did not seem to mind that he had worried Rose. He was intent on getting his belated breakfast and made sure that Tom sorted him out with some cat food, before putting the milk into his and Rose's tea. Rose warmed the pastries and they both went into the sitting room at the back.

There was definitely an autumnal chill to the air and it was too chilly to take their meal outside. Only a few days before it seemed like summer, but the crazy English weather had put paid to that idea and they were now eating inside. Rose sat in an armchair next to the fireplace facing out over the river and Tom sat on the sofa along the back wall. They gazed out over the river and across to the sea, while chomping at their pastries.

In the room above, the figurehead was mirroring their gaze and looking out in the same direction across the fields towards the sea. The telescope was also pointing the same direction and Mowzer, having eaten his breakfast, was sitting next to the figurehead gazing intently into the distance. To anyone walking along the footpath at the edge of the river it looked to all intents and purposes as if they were all waiting for someone or something.

Tom was not really looking at the scenery, he was thinking about the path he had found at the edge of the front grass. He wanted to uncover the path to see where it led. It seemed to divide the front grass in two, but both halves of the remaining garden would not be equal, so it would make a pretty crazy garden design. It was intriguing and perplexing, but it was not his garden, so he had to tread very carefully. He would have to ask Rose.

Rose gazed into the distance, she was thinking once again how lucky she was to live in this pretty little spot and was waiting for Tom to ask her for her business ideas. He had not really discussed his ideas for the property with her. She was pleased that he didn't, but slightly worried that he still had an ulterior motive. She wondered if she should ask him outright what he thought she should do with the place. If she did this she would know. She was not sure that she wanted to know either. These thoughts were spinning round her head when she heard a familiar vehicle pull up on the drive way, footsteps sounded on the gravel, and she heard a polite tap on the kitchen door.

"It's unlocked, just come in," Rose yelled, "there should be a cup of tea in the pot. We are in the back room, grab a cup and a pastry and come and join us."

There was a clatter, rattle, and a bang from the kitchen. "Don't be daft, come and join us before you look at the boiler, Steve. I'll have your guts for garters otherwise."

Steve poked his head around the door. "I would rather get on with it, but you have twisted my arm as those pastries look lovely and the pot's still warm. Can I get you both another?" Tom shook his head and grinned at Rose then at Steve.

"Really guys, am I that obvious? I would love some more please. I am starving, as I missed breakfast. I can't believe I overslept and Mowzer did not wake me up for his breakfast."

"That might have something to do with the half-eaten mouse on the back doorstep," Steve exclaimed, "he has left you the head and the tail. Looks like he has eaten the rest, that might explain why he did not cry for his breakfast this morning. Looks like he is living up to his name."

Rose squirmed inwardly; she had fancied that Mowzer had gone off on an adventure with her ghostly Captain. As if. He had caught a mouse like a good 'Mowzer' should and then, with a full tummy, sunbathed all morning on the windowsill of the bedroom.

Just then Steve added, "Why he put what remains of the mouse into that old sailor's hat I will never know! What is the hat doing outside on the back doorstep, Rose?"

Fifty-Eight

Steve checked the boiler was working properly and was not leaking water or gas, as he promised Rose in the pub the previous evening. He gave it a thorough check and then the all clear. Rose asked him to pop in again when he had some spare time, she had decided to talk through her ideas with him again. Steve had a sound business head and was very organised. His experience and expertise when project managing the work on the main house had proved his mettle to her. It was Steve that had suggested that she submit an application to change the outbuildings to business use, just in case she needed an income later on. He was also a very good friend. Rose reasoned that Tom was a very good friend too, but she was worried that the hot, steamy nights and passion would cloud his judgment. She knew that he had far too many ideas of his own that he was keeping to himself.

Steve had thrown what was left of the mouse in the bin and put the hat on the kitchen work surface before leaving. It was the sight of the hat on the work surface when she returned to the kitchen after spending a long afternoon lazing about the house with Tom, that made her thoughts return to the Captain. What would he want her to do with her inheritance?

Tom followed Rose into the kitchen and gently propelled her into the garden, steering her by the arm into the front garden, by the front door. The pile of freshly dug earth that he had pushed around with his foot earlier was still there. It looked like a mole had just arrived and another pile of dirt was imminent.

"What are you up to now, Tom?"

"I was hoping you would take a look at this and see what you think. It looks like there is path running through here. It could go in this direction," he gestured frantically with his arms, "or it could end up over there. What do you think?"

Rose looked down at her feet and mirrored his stance that she had seen earlier from the bedroom window. She shuffled her feet and kicked the dirt back and forth. "You may be right, you know. There is a path of some kind right here, but it doesn't feel like it is in the right place, it is off centre. Perhaps we should uncover it for a bit, using a spade, I think there is one over in the outbuildings somewhere. Not sure if it's mine though, it could be Steve's. I'm sure he won't mind."

Tom did not need to be asked twice. He raced over to the building and found the spade just inside the door. He raced back to Rose and started to follow the path with the spade, scrapping the grass away to one side as he went. Rose stayed by his side and watched as the path was uncovered. The path led straight into the lawn and then made an abrupt turn and started to make its way across to the other side of the garden. Tom stopped scraping and retraced his steps back to the middle where the turn started. He scraped a little to the other side as well and the path turned and made its way across the other side of the garden too. Turning back and going back to the side of the garden where he left Rose, Tom continued. The path continued too. It carried on, following a straight line before turning away at a sharp right angle back up the garden. Rose and Tom stopped and looked to see where the path was heading. The house was quite far away, and the path was leading nowhere. It did not make any sense.

"What do you make of this then?" Tom asked, looking across at Rose.

"It seems a little odd to me, but perhaps it's a path to wander around the garden and it is meant to meander a bit."

"I would have imagined it would have curved if that had been the case. It is dead straight, and it came from the front door, so I expected to head right down to the road, not veer a sharp left and right. This house and garden is a right puzzle. Nothing is what you expect."

Rose took the spade from Tom and started to peel back the grass, copying the way he had done it. The path continued in its straight trajectory and kept going and going and going. It did stop though, rather abruptly, and there was no apparent reason. None at all.

They both laughed and looked back at the path they had uncovered in such a short space of time and in such a hurry. It was such an anticlimax.

"What did you expect to find then?" Rose giggled as she glanced up at Tom.

"Oh, I was expecting to find your Captain's pot of gold, mistress," Tom said in his best nautical twang grinning from ear to ear.

"Not sure what I was expecting, but the sudden stop was a bit unexpected, not sure I want to dig for treasure now," she laughed. "Think we should call it a day and think on it a while. My mum always said you need to sleep on it and you will find the answers in the morning. That's what we should do."

It was starting to get dark as Rose and Tom finished in the garden and when they returned to the house, they had to switch the lights on as the house was in darkness. Mowzer was curled up on the kitchen work surface in his hat and did not stir even when the room was illuminated by light. Rose bustled about cooking dinner and left

Mowzer right there fast asleep. Then, Rose and Tom ate from trays on their laps in the back room, they talked about a great many things, but Rose did not mention her business plans and Tom did not prompt her. Rose had enjoyed her lazy day and did not want to spoil it. She was hoping that Tom would stay the night and keep her company.

Fifty-Nine

Rose spent the next few days worrying about her decision to pack in her job in London. Tom was busy with a garden project in Sussex and was working away from home for a few days, so she had no one to distract her from her worries. Mowzer had disappeared again as well. Rose had searched all over the house and in all the outbuildings, but Mowzer was nowhere to be found. She had even made a frantic phone call to Tom asking him to check the back of his van and in his client's garden just in case Mowzer had hitched a ride.

Tom had looked everywhere too, but Mowzer was most definitely missing again.

So, Rose sat and drank endless cups of tea – a sure way to waste some time – until her mind settled, and she reached for her laptop and started to make notes of all her ideas to make money and keep her treasured Captain's House. She thought of ways to market the house, if she wanted to explore the bed and breakfast option, like her good friend Val. However, she only had two spare bedrooms in the house and really disliked the thought of a strangers sleeping in the rooms next to hers. She could convert her outbuildings into bedrooms or even separate accommodation for guests with en suite bathrooms and cooking facilities.

Alternatively, the outbuildings could be rented out to store equipment for Steve and the other workman that had worked on the house renovation. They were always complaining that they had nowhere to store anything and constantly worried about keeping their expensive tools in their work vans. Another idea was to convert the outbuildings into separate units for individual businesses.

Now the ideas were in black and white, Rose felt happier. She was taking control of the situation and her worries and intended to cost out each idea, adding a list of pros and cons to help her decide. The biggest decision to be made at this moment in time was whether to discuss her plans with anyone new or to mull them over until she was sure.

Her mum and dad would give her advice, but it would be biased in order to protect her investment and they would ensure that there would be little or no element of risk. Rose wanted to spend time in her new property and be able to have a reasonably decent lifestyle as well. The last thing she wanted was to commute to London at silly o'clock and return to the house at an indecent hour. This would mean that she would only spend any real time at the house at the weekends. It was an irrational way to think, Rose had only lived in the house for a short time, but she already thought she had always belonged there and felt so at home. As if it was meant to be. A bizarre sentiment, Rose wouldn't be anywhere if she could not afford to live there. As Doreen was facing the ordeal of selling her pub and her livelihood because she could not make ends meet, Rose did not want to join her. She really felt for Doreen and her heart lurched when she had passed The Ship and saw the 'For Sale' sign in the pub garden. It made her predicament all the more real.

Her house was nearly finished and just needed Rose to add all the finishing touches and make yet more decisions like the colour of the walls or if she wanted the tiles replacing in the bathroom, on the kitchen floor … The list was endless.

All Rose seemed to do recently was sit and drink tea and gaze into

666666

666

the distance, wondering about this and that and jumping from one job to another, one decision to another, and procrastinating about everything. Other times she would drink wine, eat chocolate, or stuff herself full of the ultimate comfort foods, cake, chips, and takeaways.

In the end, the indecision drove her mad and she reached for her mobile. She had sat and pondered for too long and she was cross with herself for doing precisely nothing. She dialed and waited for the call to be answered. The call was answered immediately and after Rose had said the customary 'Hi', there was a long pause, followed by a long sigh.

"Oh, it's you."

"Who were you expecting?" asked Rose.

"I was expecting Patrick to call me and ask me out any time now," replied Lisa, with another dramatic sigh. "I guess I will have to wait a while longer."

"Who, may I ask, is Patrick? Have you got your eyes on a new fella?"

"Nearly. Almost. Just waiting for him to call and ask me on a date. I thought you might have been him. Not that I am not pleased to hear from you. You still seeing Tom, or have you had second thoughts and are dating the delectable Steve instead? Or are you stringing both of them along to see which one is better in bed?"

"Whoo, Lisa, you have got it bad. You need to leave all that man stuff behind for a while. Fancy a weekend with me to get away from it all for a bit? I could use some company and some advice."

"Well, I have always liked that Steve, if you want my advice. Tom is a bit too mysterious and too good to be true. I guess you could be swayed by their sexual prowess as well!"

"I was talking about my business plans and financial security actually. What's that Patrick's number and I will call him myself and get him to wine and dine you and take you to bed. You might be more sensible then!"

Both of them collapsed into fits of giggles and snorts and eventually Lisa caught her breath.

"You know what, I will be there this weekend, I have so missed you. Patrick can wait."

"Are you sure?"

"Oh yeah, treat them mean and keep them keen, is that what they say? Pick me up Saturday morning, I will get the same train as last time, unless I have a late night …" with that pregnant pause, Lisa hung up.

Sixty

When the weekend arrived, and Lisa and Rose got together, like all good friends, it was as if they had never been apart. They fell into easy conversation immediately. Rose was struck by how nice it was to speak freely without having to think first. To worry about the effect that her words would have on other people. She adored Tom but was always wondering if he was too good to be true. His fascination with her house delighted her and worried her in turn. She tended to think before she spoke with him and still could not shake of the belief that he was only really interested in the house, not her. However, his affection for her seemed very real.

She found herself describing the evening she had spent with Tom uncovering the pathway in the garden.

"It was so exciting finding the path, but then it just stopped as suddenly as it started, so mysterious, just like Tom."

"Where is Tom this weekend?" Lisa asked.

"He is working away, and the job was not finished as quickly as he had hoped, he is staying on a few days in the hope of finishing it by the beginning of next week. It wasn't helped by the spell of heavy rain we had at the end of the week."

"I am just second best then," Lisa retorted with a quick toss of her head, "you had nothing better to do, as you are now a lady of leisure, or are you a lady who lunches?"

"I need to sort out a business plan very soon or I won't be the lady of this house at all. My inheritance will not last forever, that's really what you are here for – my cunning plan."

"All girls together then to talk over your future plans. We need to get some wine, chocolate, and nibbles to sort that out. I think we should put some comfy chairs in the back bedroom and sit looking out at the sea for inspiration with that other female house guest of yours. The figurehead, have you given her a name yet? Or do you know her name and the ship she was part of? The one thing for certain is that she was connected to your ghostly captain in some way, and she suits this house to a T."

"You want to sit and look out over to the sea, why don't we do that downstairs? Tell me again why are we moving stuff about? You are not going all weird on me again, are you?"

The last time Lisa had visited the property she had gone off into her own dream world from time to time, prompted by all manner of things. Lisa was a dreamy girl by character, but the effect on Lisa's personality and mood was quite pronounced the last time she was there. Rose wasn't sure whether to be excited or worried about Lisa's suggestion.

The view was better upstairs and two comfy chairs, one either side of the telescope, sitting in the square bay looked very cosy and very right for the space. The bed was pushed up against the wall and now looked out of place. The room made a terrific upstairs sitting room. The view was so much better upstairs. Rose and Lisa had manhandled the chairs into place and her bedroom looked like something was missing without the chair in the window. The stories of the Captain's ghost looking out at passersby in the lane were all prompted by the Captain's jacket hanging on the corner of the chair. It had fooled Rose herself many a time when she had arrived home and thought someone was watching her from the window.

Lisa had gone very quiet; she had the Captain's jacket in her hands. She stood leaning against the chair, looking out at the distant sea. She swayed from side to side, her body taking on the movement of the ocean, as if she was standing on the deck of a ship not the solid floorboards of the house.

Rose looked across at her friend and saw her eyes starting to glaze over and grabbed her quick. She pulled her towards her and then manhandled her into the armchair. For all intents and purposes, it looked like she had fainted. Rose felt for her pulse and it was steady and strong. She sat down at Lisa's feet and held on to her knees. She was not sure what to do, but wanted to hold Lisa, to reassure her that she was there. Then, suddenly, Lisa, sat up and looked around.

"I don't remember sitting down and what are you doing cuddling my knees?" she giggled.

"You fainted, I think, sweetie. Are you feeling all right now?" questioned Rose, with a frown on her face. She loved her best friend dearly and was beginning to get worried about these strange lapses.

She was worried about her own fainting episode in the antique shop, but she never mentioned it and had pushed that to the back of her mind and not told anyone. She had hidden the telescope away as well, as she was frightened that it could trigger something unexplained again.

Lisa retorted, "I felt like I was standing on the deck of a ship. I could feel the sway of the ocean underneath me. The room faded from sight and I was sure that someone was trying to speak to me, they were trying to say something very important. The words were very faint, but the voice was very insistent. The message I am very sure was urgent. Very urgent. Then I felt a pressure on my knees and there you were. Right there with that silly expression in your eyes, as if you expected me to drop dead! I am fine, you silly woman. Why don't you do something useful and pop the kettle on?"

"Yeah, why don't we have a nice cup of tea. But I'm not sure I want to leave you up here on your own now. Do you want to join me? I think I have something nice tucked away in the cupboard for you. One of those chocolate cakes from the local bakery that you raved about last time you visited. It turns out Val wasn't the baker after all. She finally told me a couple of weeks ago when she got tipsy at the pub for her birthday. Would you believe it?"

Lisa gazed at her friend and made a big effort to smile. She wanted to reassure herself and Rose that she was fine, but she was anything but. She felt sick, her stomach was churning, and her head ached badly. How could she tell her friend she felt sick, the same as she got whenever she travelled on a boat? She was seasick, but she was still on firm ground, albeit a house that resembled a boat. Why wasn't Rose, the one that got seasick? The Captain was her ancestor and the house her inheritance. Very strange.

Sixty-One

Perched on the edge of the tiny work bench in the kitchen with her legs crossed untidily, Lisa poked at her chocolate cake with her fork and pushed it around her plate. Rose had given her a huge wedge of cake as she had quite a reputation for consuming cake in large quantities. Lisa could not eat a morsel. Her stomach was churning, and the house would not keep still around her. It kept moving.

Across the kitchen, Rose looked on in a matronly fashion. She could see that her friend was having trouble keeping it all together and was not eating her cake, merely toying with it. Gently, without saying a word, she took the plate from her and placed it on the work top.

"Quite a mess you have made of the cake, but you haven't eaten a bite. You don't need to tell me that you are feeling out of sorts. I can see that. Perhaps you had better lie down for a bit."

Lisa wanted to disagree with her friend and snatch her cake back and tell Rose she was being so silly, but she did not have the energy. She allowed herself to be led back upstairs and tucked up into bed without a murmur. Everything felt heavy, her arms, legs, and head. She sank into the mattress and her eyes closed. She drifted away into a deep, dreamless sleep.

Meanwhile, Rose sat in one of the armchairs and watched her friend sleeping, trying to make sense of it all. The house affected everyone that spent time in it. Most people felt something. The Captain's hat seemed to have a mind of its own and Mowzer was still missing. She wondered if Lisa was dreaming about the sea and the Captain. She hoped that when she awoke she would have something new to tell her. The house and its mysterious Captains seemed to want to convey a message. Or was Lisa just receptive to past conversations and happenings at the house and was picking up bits and pieces of random information?

The truth of the matter was probably that Lisa was working far too hard, putting in long hours at work and playing with equal intensity as well. She was just tired, and her mind was playing tricks on her. Rose had not helped by constantly regaling her with tales of the Captain and stories of his ghostly presence.

Now that Lisa was sleeping peacefully, Rose left her alone and traipsed down the stairs and out into the garden to look for Mowzer. She carried his box of cat crunchies and shook them every couple of paces to try and entice him out from his hiding place. She tramped up and down the garden, peeking behind shrubs and bushes and in the front hedge. It was there, hidden in the hedge, she found the wooden sign, tucked behind a stout branch. It was a couple of feet long and there was the faint outline of a name. Rose pulled it out of the undergrowth and took it into the house to clean it up and have a good look at it.

She laid it on the kitchen worktop next to the mangled piece of uneaten chocolate cake and tore a strip of kitchen towel to wipe the dirt of it, wetting it first under the cold tap. Gently she rubbed at the wood with the damp towel and the dirt was displaced and slowly the name became clearer.

There was the name of her house. Right there. Just has she had always known it.

'The Captain's House'.

So, everyone was right, a Captain had lived here all along.

Sixty-Two

Rose could not settle. Lisa's words started to bounce around inside her head. She already doubted Tom, but she was getting that nagging feeling more and more frequently. Rose scribbled a note for her friend, next to the remains of the mangled cake, and grabbed her car keys.

On sheer impulse she decided to pay a visit to Tom's brother. On the way, Rose thought about the two guys in her life. Rose really enjoyed Steve's company. Steve was a normal, hard-working guy who clearly thought a great deal of her, and she really liked him. He was fun to be around, and she already trusted him. It was Steve she called, not Tom, when she moved the valuable paintings. Both Steve and Tom had work vans, so either of them could have done the job, but she did not want to ask Tom. Part of her did not want Tom or anyone else to know where the paintings were being kept for the time being. Mike had made her very wary. Tom just seemed too good to be true!

Rose managed to get a table outside overlooking the sea when she arrived at the restaurant. Joe was working out at the back when she arrived so he was unaware that she was there for a while. She was eating her main course by the time Joe discovered her. He was surprised to see her dining alone.

"What have you done with Tom?" he asked. Rose had not made any arrangements with Tom for this evening and was eating alone and told Joe this.

Joe took one look at her shy, pensive smile and sat down on the other side of the table.

"You and Tom are moving fast, aren't you. It's not his way and I can see by your face it is not yours either. You are not here just for the amazing food, are you? Are you here to see me?" he asked.

Rose nodded, "It is all too good to be true and he is the first guy that I have ever fallen for so hard and so fast. There must something there, something that I don't know."

"Let me fill you in with some background. Tom is quiet and shy. He is much more at home with plants and nature than girls. I am just as surprised as you that you have got it together so quick. Tom is shy with girls and does not trust females at all. He has only had one steady girlfriend. She spent all his money and then dumped him for his best mate. It took him a long time to get over that. You know he spent all his teenage years, as did I, working in gardens and restaurants. We were going to run a hotel together when we grew up, Tom dealing with the outside stuff and me running the kitchen and housekeeping, but we grew apart as brothers do. We both started businesses but not together. We both work hard and that is all Tom and I have done for years. He worked very hard at horticultural college and for other people before he started making a go of it himself. Tom has always liked your Captain's House, he spent hours in the garden as a boy, when the rest of us were on the beach. It was one of the places that he drew inspiration from when we used to dream about a hotel by the sea, 'just like the Captain's House', he used to say."

"Oh yeah," said Rose when he had finished. "So, Tom could be after my Captain's House and not me after all. Someone else after my inheritance and good fortune. The hotel of his dreams, not his dream girl, she just comes with the place!"

Rose put her knife and fork down on the table and grabbed her napkin to wipe her eyes. Joe took her hands and shook them gently.

"Listen to me, Rose, do not tar my brother with the same brush as whoever it is that has hurt you. Tom thinks the world of you and speaks of you constantly. He loves you, not the house, I am sure."

Later, Rose drove back to the Captain's House in deadly silence. She did not even switch the radio on to keep her company in the car, as was her habit when it was dark. Her thoughts were racing, and she could not make sense of anything. Perhaps she should sell this house and go back to town and get a little house in suburbia with the money it made. She drove into the drive, turned the engine off, and just sat looking at the house from the car. Keeping her distance from the house that had made her so happy, which was now making her so miserable as everyone wants the house or its valuable contents, not her.

Mowzer jumped onto the bonnet and peered anxiously at her through the windscreen. She had been crying and Mowzer was picking up her distress. He paced up and down the bonnet and started to claw at the glass to get through to her. Rose clambered out of the car and bent down and picked up the kitten for a cuddle. She looked up at the house and could not help but smile. Her moment of anxiety had passed. There was no way she was selling her Captain's House. She vowed to be a happy spinster with her handsome cat, Mowzer, and not to worry about men in her life. Perhaps she would give Steve another chance. There was not the passion there right now, but there was an enduring friendship that could be an excellent foundation.

As Rose put the key in the lock and turned it, she felt faint. The house kept coming in and out of focus. She leant against the door frame for support. Her legs felt wobbly, and she dropped an indignant Mowzer, but he was not hurt and landed on his feet. He jumped up onto the bannister at the bottom of the stairs and was then eye level with Rose. Rose tried to focus on Mowzer and kept getting lost in the deep yellow of his eyes. His eyes were bright in the darkness and Rose was feeling more and more lightheaded. She managed to climb the stairs and made it to the bed. She slumped across the eiderdown and fell into a deep sleep.

The Captain's House haunted her dreams, but the house was larger and grander. The garden was bigger too, it was beautiful. A rose garden. Roses were everywhere, in the curtains, upholstery and wallpaper. Every so often, Rose glimpsed a shadow; sometimes male, sometimes female. The mistress of the house was mainly in the shadows. She held a bunch of roses in one hand and a beautiful china vase in the other. Then she faded away. The Captain was once more in her dreams, in different uniforms, sometimes clean shaven, other times with a big, bushy beard always with a sailor's hat on his head or in his hands. The face was warm, friendly, and oh so familiar.

Rose awoke with a start and looked around in the semi darkness. Rose had seen the face of the Captain and she tried desperately not to forget him. Her dreams were vivid and left her trembling and ever so slightly scared. Mowzer was nowhere to be seen. Rose had to find him to check he was all right. She thought he was probably sleeping in his Captain's hat, but the hat was empty on the chair. As she stumbled past the hat it fell to the floor. Rose picked it up and carried it with her, pulling it to her for comfort.

As Rose reached the top of the stairs, she was bare foot, she must have slipped her shoes off in her sleep. Her feet felt something gritty and rough underfoot. Rose looked down and she saw a trail of sand from her bedroom door, flowing down the stairs. Rose broke into a run. She ran down the stairs and pushed the front door wide open. The sand continued. Rose followed the trail. It led into the middle of the garden.

The garden was back in its prime, just as it was in the painting of the garden. There were lots and lots of beautiful roses, all in full bloom. As she walked past, her body touched the roses and they started to grow and tangle together, shielding the path from view and forcing her to push past them, the thorns caught in her clothes and scratched her skin. The wind started to gust and tore the petals from the roses. It created a billowing swirl of petals and leaves, which clouded her vision, making it difficult to see where she was going and follow the trail of sand.

She had to stop. The roses were blocking her way entirely. She gazed up in despair, waving her arms to clear the way. Her hands groped in the air and were almost immediately filled with petals. She was surrounded by the roses and their petals were falling on her like snowflakes. She caught her breath at the beauty of the roses and felt her mind and body grow still. She closed her eyes and felt a serene kind of peace wash over her. When she opened her eyes, the morning light was getting stronger. The roses were back to their neglected beauty and the shower of rose petals had stopped.

She could now see that the sandy trail was leading to the bench in the garden. The wind died down completely, the garden was so still. She gazed across to the bench, peering hesitantly through the mist of the morning, still clutching the rose petals in her hands. There was a heady scent of roses in the air all around her, a strong smell, far stronger than that of a single rose.

In front of her, sitting on the bench, gazing in the distance towards the sea, she saw her Captain once again in the fading shadows; however, sitting beside him, oblivious to the Captain's presence, was Tom.

The two men in her life were sitting together. They were uncannily alike.

The Captain and Tom became aware of Rose in the garden and smiled at her together, as one. The Captain turned towards Tom and nodded his head in farewell, his eyes then met hers and he held her gaze as he vanished. Her Captain sitting beside Tom was all the proof that she needed. When the Captain had nodded his head to Tom, to say farewell, he was conveying his approval as well. She was certain of it. They both loved her, it was very clear by the way they both looked at her. She felt it too. It was then that she knew for sure that she loved Tom.

Just as she loves her Captain and his mysterious house.

Some weeks later, Rose wandered down to the churchyard to look for any sign of her ghostly Captain amongst the graves. It was something she had meant to do earlier when she had first arrived in the village after inheriting the house. Hidden in the undergrowth she discovered the gravestone she had been looking for. There was an inscription engraved on the stone, which read:

Captain Nathaniel Petts, 1865-1948
Together again with his adored wife, Rose Petts, 1870-1946

Beneath the two names the familiar phrase, 'I venture across the seas, but always return to you,' was carved into the stone. She touched her ring that bore the same inscription. She felt a presence across her shoulders as if someone had their arm around her. It tightened. The weight lifted, and she felt a slight nudge on her arm. Then, it was gone.

ABOUT THE AUTHOR

Mel J Wallis lives in Kent and has based her Captain trilogy in the Kent county. She lives in a village on the North Downs with her husband, Andy, and two daughters, Amy and Louise. She shares her home with the family's two cats, Pickle and Kitty, and the garden with their two rabbits, Toffee and Apple.

She enjoys walking the Kent countryside, deep in thought, contemplating her plotlines and developing her characters. In the summer you will find her stretched out in the sunshine in her garden and in the winter curled up in a comfy chair in front of the fire, always with a book in her hands.

She loves to wander around antique and second-hand book shops, searching for inspiration and treasure. Soaking up the unique musty smell of old books and trying not to spend too much. She has similar problems in a garden centre looking at plants and trying desperately not to bring them home. Her home is packed with books and her garden stuffed with all manner of plants. She constantly tries to declutter the house or the garden in some semblance of order when she takes a break from writing.

She is a passionate volunteer and supporter of several hearing loss charities, in particular Hearing Link and Hearing Dogs for Deaf People. Living with hearing loss all her life, she is now incredibly lucky to be partnered with her very own Hearing Dog, Lucy, to share her life with.

She was inspired to write 'The Captain's House' after glimpsing a mysterious empty house out of the corner of her eye while driving past on the way to the beach with the children one day. 'The Captain's House' is her first novel and the first in the Captain trilogy.

Printed in Great Britain
by Amazon

84034789R00153